"Get some rest. You want to be alert when we make a break for it tonight."

"Will you rest, too?" she asked.

"I'll keep watch," he said. "I won't let anything happen to you."

He buried his face in her hair and inhaled deeply of her floral-and-spice scent. She made him feel more vulnerable than he ever had, yet at the same time stronger. A man who had spent his life avoiding complications, he welcomed the challenges she brought. She made him think what the future might look like with her in it.

She stirred, and he pushed away his musings. She opened her eyes, then smiled. "Does this mean the wonderful dream I was having is real?" she asked.

"What was the dream?"

Her smile widened. "It involved a big feather bed and you and me—naked."

He indulged himself with a kiss, fighting the urge to take her there on the hard ground. "We'll have to see about making that dream come true later."

BLACK CANYON CONSPIRACY

CINDI MYERS

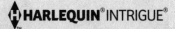

HARLEQUIN® INTRIGUE®

For the Western Slope Writers of RMFW

Recycling programs
for this product may
not exist in your area.

ISBN-13: 978-0-373-74911-9

Black Canyon Conspiracy

Copyright © 2015 by Cynthia Myers

Printed in U.S.A.

www.Harlequin.com

Cindi Myers is an author of more than fifty novels. When she's not crafting new romance plots, she enjoys skiing, gardening, cooking, crafting and daydreaming. A lover of small-town life, she lives with her husband and two spoiled dogs in the Colorado mountains.

Books by Cindi Myers

The Ranger Brigade

The Guardian
Lawman Protection
Colorado Bodyguard
Black Canyon Conspiracy

Harlequin Intrigue

Rocky Mountain Revenge
Rocky Mountain Rescue

Harlequin Heartwarming

Her Cowboy Soldier
What She'd Do for Love

Visit the Author Profile page at Harlequin.com for more titles.

CAST OF CHARACTERS

Lauren Starling—The former television news star has escaped the man who was holding her captive, only to find her reputation in tatters and her life turned upside down. Diagnosed six months before with bipolar disorder, Lauren struggles to stay on an even keel while fighting an unseen enemy who wants her dead.

Marco Cruz—The former Special Forces soldier turned DEA agent, and a member of the Ranger Brigade, has a reputation for being cool and ruthless. He rescued Lauren from Richard Prentice once, but being with Marco could be even more dangerous to her peace of mind.

Richard Prentice—The billionaire held Lauren prisoner on his ranch for six weeks, but he's managed to persuade authorities that she was a willing guest and her captivity was a figment of her troubled mind. Now that she's free of his control, he may have decided to do away with her for good.

The Ranger Brigade—An interagency task force of law enforcement officers charged with fighting crime on public lands in southwest Colorado, including Black Canyon of the Gunnison National Park, Curecanti Wilderness Area and Gunnison Gorge Wilderness Area.

Phillip Starling—Lauren's ex-husband, an out-of-work actor, somehow found the money for an expensive drug rehab program. He may know a lot more about Richard Prentice's connections than he's saying.

Sophie Montgomery—Lauren's sister worked hard to locate Lauren when she disappeared, but how long will she be willing to put her life on hold?

Bruno Adel—Who is the military man in the mysterious photo, and what is his connection to Richard Prentice?

Chapter One

The sound of the explosion reverberated through the underground tunnels. Lauren tried to run, terrified the rocks would collapse around her, but her legs felt as if they were mired in sand. She fought to see in the murky darkness, choking on rising dust, her ears ringing from the aftershock. She opened her mouth to scream, but no sound emerged.

A strong hand grabbed hers, pulling her toward the light. Gunshots sounded behind them, even as rock chips flew from the wall beside her head, the fragments stinging her skin. The man with her pulled her in front of him, shielding her with his body. "Go!" he commanded, and shoved her harder. "Run!"

She ran, dodging piles of rubble and fresh cascades of rock. The dim light ahead began to grow brighter. Footsteps pounded behind her and she started to scream again, but it was only the man, his embrace warm and reassuring.

"It's going to be all right," he said. "You're strong. You can make it."

He sounded so certain that, despite all the evidence to the contrary, she believed him.

Another tremor shook the cavern, and larger boulders crashed around them. One struck her shoulder, knocking her to her knees. The man pulled her up, into his arms, and kept running, dodging the falling rock, taking the blows and moving on, always forward, toward freedom.

The cool night air washing over her brought tears to her eyes. She stared at the blurred stars overhead and choked back a sob. The first stars she'd seen in weeks. A taste of freedom she'd feared she might never know again.

"Can you walk?" the man asked, setting her on her feet, but keeping his arm firmly around her, supporting her.

She nodded. "I can."

"Then, we've got to go. We've got to stop him."

Hand in hand, they raced toward the castle situated improbably in the middle of the Colorado desert. She seemed to fly over the ground, her feet not touching it, only the firm grip of the man's hand in hers anchoring her to the earth.

She heard the helicopter before she saw it, the steady *whump! whump!* of the rotors beat-

ing the air. Then they ascended a small hill
and stared at the chopper lifting off, soaring
into the pink clouds of dawn. *No!* she silently
screamed.

LOUD, OUT-OF-TUNE CHIMES from the doorbell
pulled Lauren from the dream—one she'd had
too often in the weeks since her escape from
the abandoned mine that had been her prison
for almost a month. The details sometimes
changed, but the results were the same as reality—her captor, Richard Prentice, escaping
into the night as she watched, powerless.

"I don't think she's awake yet," she heard
her sister, Sophie, tell whoever was at the door.

Lauren struggled into a sitting position and
checked the clock. Almost eleven. How had she
slept so late? "I'm awake," she called. "Give me
a minute to get dressed."

She threw back the covers and sat up. She
was safe in the apartment she shared with her
sister in Montrose, Colorado. The words of her
rescuer still echoed from the dream. *You're
strong. You can make it.*

In the living room, she found Sophie with
two other women. Emma Wade, a tall redhead
who dressed to show off her curves in flowing skirts and high heels, stood beside Abby
Stewart, a sweet grad student whose shoulder-

length brown hair was cut to hide most of the scar on one cheek, the result of a wound she'd received while in the army in Afghanistan. The two women had befriended first Sophie, then Lauren, after the sisters' arrival in Montrose.

"Sorry to disturb you, but we've got something here you need to see." Emma handed Lauren a newspaper. "Maybe you'd better sit down before you read it."

"What is it?" Sophie asked, and followed Lauren to the couch, where Lauren sat and focused on the newspaper, nausea quickly rising in her throat as she read the headline.

Former Top News Anchor Released read the headline on the small article in the *Denver Post*'s entertainment section.

Lauren Starling, twice voted most popular news anchor in the *Post*'s annual "best of" selections, has been released from her contract with station KQUE, effective immediately. Station president Ross Carmichael asked for the public's support and understanding for Ms. Starling "at this difficult time. Lauren's illness is affecting her ability to perform her job, so we thought it was in her best interest to release her from her obligations, to allow her time to seek treatment and recover," he said.

In March of this year, Starling was diagnosed with bipolar disorder, following several incidences of erratic behavior on-air. She made headlines when she disappeared for several weeks in May and June, eventually turning up at a ranch owned by billionaire developer Richard Prentice. Starling has accused Prentice of kidnapping her, a charge he denies. He says he offered his home as a safe place for Starling, a longtime family friend, to heal and recover.

Starling's former husband, actor Phillip Starling, also issued a statement regarding Starling's accusations against Prentice. "Lauren hasn't been herself for the past year," he told this reporter. "Her wild accusations against Richard—a man we've both known for years—prove how unstable she has become. I hope for her sake she will seek treatment and I wish her all the best."

Ms. Starling was unavailable for comment.

Lauren smoothed her hand over the paper, trying to hide the shaking. She could feel the eyes of the others on her. Were they searching for signs that she was finally cracking up? She was used to people looking at her. She'd been a cheerleader and a beauty queen, and had finally landed her dream job of prime-time news anchor at Denver's number two station. She'd spent most of her life seeking and gaining attention.

But that was when the looks from others had been admiring, even envious. Now people regarded her with suspicion. The looks came attached to labels. She was "unstable" or "erratic" or "crazy." She'd admitted she had a problem and gotten help, but instead of sympathy and understanding, she'd only earned suspicion. She didn't know how to handle the stares anymore.

"Lauren, are you okay?"

Sophie, her sister, asked the question the rest of them had probably been wondering. Lauren fixed a bright smile on her face and tossed her head back, defiant. "I'm fine."

"I'm so sorry," Emma, who worked as a reporter for the *Post*, said. "I hated to be the bearer of bad news, but I didn't want you hearing about it from someone who wasn't a friend, either."

"I can't believe Phil would say something like that." Sophie rubbed Lauren's shoulder, just as she had when they were girls and Lauren had suffered a nightmare. "I never did like the guy."

Lauren had loved Phil; maybe part of her still did. Handsome and charming, as outgoing as she was and a talented actor, Phil had seemed the perfect match for her. But maybe two big egos in a marriage hadn't been a good idea. Or maybe he'd sensed something was broken in her long before she'd discovered the reason for her erratic mood swings and out-of-control emotions. When he'd finally come clean about cheating on her with a woman he worked with, she'd taken the news badly. Though in the end, that plunge into depression had led to the diagnosis and work to get her life under control.

"Prentice probably paid Phil off." Abby scowled at the paper. "And now he's using his influence to ruin your reputation."

"So far he's doing a pretty good job." She flipped the paper over and started to fold it, but another headline caught her eye. "Oh, no!" she moaned.

"I didn't want you to see that." Emma tried to pull the paper away, but Sophie took it instead.

"'Task Force Status in Jeopardy,'" Sophie read.

"'Senator Peter Mattheson has called for a Senate hearing to consider disbanding the interagency task force responsible for solving crimes on public lands in the region around Black Canyon of the Gunnison National Park. The task force, more commonly known as The Ranger Brigade, has successfully stopped a drug smuggling and human trafficking ring in the area as well as solved other less sensational crimes, but recently made headlines over charges of harassment brought by billionaire developer Richard Prentice. Prentice, not a stranger to controversies involving various government agencies, filed suit earlier this year against the Rangers, demanding seven billion dollars in damages.'"

"Don't read any more," Abby said. "It's all a bunch of lies."

"This is so awful," Lauren said. "There should be something we can do to stop this guy."

"The Rangers are working harder than ever to do just that," Emma said. "I'm worried Graham is going to work himself right into a heart attack." Captain Graham Ellison, FBI agent and Emma's fiancé, headed up The Ranger Brigade. Other members of the task force included

Abby's boyfriend, Michael Dance, and Sophie's boyfriend, Rand Knightbridge.

"What will happen if the task force disbands?" Lauren asked.

"It won't," Emma said. "All of Richard Prentice's money isn't going to keep him out of jail forever. The grand jury is supposed to end its proceedings today. Once they hand down an indictment, all his money and influence won't mean anything."

"*If* they hand down an indictment," Abby said. "Michael is afraid all the expensive experts Prentice has hired will persuade the grand jury that he's as innocent and persecuted as he likes to portray himself in the press."

"They can't ignore all the evidence against him," Lauren said. She had spent two full days last week in the grand jury room, giving every detail of her six weeks as Prentice's captive, as well as information about the investigation she'd conducted into his affairs that had led the billionaire to capture her and hide her away, first upstairs in his mansion, then in an abandoned mine on his property.

"Michael says he heard Prentice hired an expert to testify that the picture you gave them of Prentice with Alan Milbanks was so blurry no one could tell who the men in the photo really were," Abby said.

"Alan Milbanks gave me that photograph himself before he died," Lauren said. The drug dealer had been shot to death in the fish store that served as a front for his smuggling operation only a few days before Lauren was rescued. "He told me Richard Prentice was bankrolling his drug business."

Abby shrugged. "I'm just saying that some people are more easily persuaded than others. The jury might believe Prentice."

They might. After all, Lauren had believed his lies, too, at least at first. He'd portrayed himself as a caring, charity-minded businessman who'd been forced, by circumstance, into the role of champion of individual rights. All his problems with the government were simply misunderstandings, or the result of his defense of personal liberty for everyone.

"I heard the grand jury brought in a lot of other experts," Emma said. "Of course, it's all hush-hush. No one is supposed to know who testifies before the grand jury, and there isn't even a judge present, just the prosecutor. But people talk."

"What kind of experts?" Sophie asked.

"Psychiatrists." Emma glanced at Lauren, then quickly averted her gaze.

"I'm betting they weren't talking about Richard's state of mind," Lauren said.

"You don't know that," Sophie said. "Maybe they were explaining what would lead a man with more money than Midas to want to gain even more illegally. Or why a man known for dating models and actresses would decide to hold you hostage until you agreed to marry him."

"The psychiatrists were talking about me," Lauren said. "I saw some of the jurors' faces when I told them Richard wanted to marry me. They thought I made the whole story up." After all, that had been Prentice's defense from the moment she was found: Lauren had come to him for help. She'd always been free to leave his property, but she'd fixated on him and insisted on staying. He'd only been trying to be a good friend; the poor woman was delusional.

"All I know is that the grand jury is supposed to deliver its decision this morning and I have to get to the courthouse." Emma pulled her sunglasses from her purse. "I've already started working on my story for the next issue of the *Post*. There's no way twenty-three people could hear what happened to you, Lauren, and not indict."

"Call when you know something," Abby said.

"Oh, I will," Emma said. "We might even have

to break out a bottle of champagne, once Prentice is safely behind bars."

No one said anything until Emma had left, then Abby turned to Lauren. "Let's forget about Prentice for a little bit," she said. "What are you going to do about your job?"

Her job. For a moment she'd almost forgotten the original reason her friends had shown up this morning. She'd loved the excitement of reporting on breaking news and the feeling that she was involved in important events, a part of the lives of the people who tuned in every day to hear what she had to say. She still couldn't believe she'd lost all of that. "I guess I need a plan, huh?" Though she hadn't the foggiest idea what that plan should be.

"I think you should hire a lawyer," Abby said. "The station can't cut you off with no severance or benefits or anything when they've outright admitted their firing you is related to your medical diagnosis. The Americans with Disabilities Act probably has something to say about that."

"Abby is right," Sophie said. "Threaten to sue them and make them cough up a settlement—and continue your medical benefits, at least until you find something better."

Right. She didn't want to lose the benefits

that paid for the medication that was keeping her on an even keel. "Good idea," she said. "I have a lawyer friend in Denver. I'll call him today." She grabbed a notebook from the counter that separated the apartment's kitchen from the living area and wrote that down. It felt good to have something constructive to do.

"And I'm not going to stop going after Richard Prentice, either," she said. "Even with the grand jury indictment, the prosecutor will need every bit of evidence he can get to convict. Prentice thinks his money puts him above the law. I'm going to show him he's wrong."

"Emma will help, I'm sure," Sophie said. "If you both use your skills as investigative reporters, you're bound to turn up something."

"We can all help," Abby said. "I only know about botany, but I'm good at following directions, so if you give me a job, I'll do it." A graduate student, Abby had almost completed her work toward a master's degree in environmental science.

"Me, too," Sophie said. A former government administrator in Madison, Wisconsin, Sophie had given up her job to move to Montrose and search for Lauren.

"Thanks, all of you." Lauren hugged them each in turn. For all the terrible things that had happened to her in the past weeks and months, she'd gained these wonderful friends. They had rallied around her since she'd come to Montrose, and treated her like another sister. That was a blessing she was truly grateful for.

A knock sounded on the door. Sophie said, "That's probably Rand. He said he was going to stop by and take me to lunch."

Lauren answered the door. "Hello, Rand." She smiled at the handsome, muscular man with short brown hair who stood on the landing, then looked past him to the darker, taller man behind him. "Hello, Marco."

"How are you doing, Lauren?" Agent Marco Cruz asked as he followed his coworker into the apartment. His deep, soft voice made her heart beat a little faster. When had she turned into such a cliché, going all swoony over the handsome guy in uniform who'd just happened to save her life? Of course, pretty much any straight woman with a pulse got a little weak-kneed around Marco, who might have been the inspiration for the description "tall, dark and handsome."

But Lauren was not any woman, she told herself. She wasn't going to allow hormones to let her make a fool of herself over a guy who was probably used to women falling at his feet.

She was grateful to him, of course, but she refused to be that cliché. "I'm holding my own. Come on in."

She ushered the men into the house. Rand greeted Sophie with a kiss. Since the two had worked together to rescue Lauren, they'd been almost inseparable. "Are we interrupting something?" he asked, looking around the kitchen at the women.

"We were discussing Richard Prentice's latest," Sophie said. "Emma just left. She showed us an article in the *Post*—he's managed to get Lauren fired."

"The article doesn't say anything about Prentice getting me fired," Lauren said.

"No, but I'd bet my last dime that he paid your ex to say you were unstable," Sophie said. "And he probably threatened to sue the station if they didn't let you go."

"Prentice must have a whole team of lawyers working full-time," Rand said.

"We saw that he's suing the Rangers, and his senator friend is agitating to disband the task force," Abby said.

Rand shrugged. "Nothing new there."

"Do you think he'll succeed in breaking you up?" Sophie asked.

"I don't think so. He's just trying to distract attention away from his own troubles."

"Emma told us the grand jury plans to hand down an indictment today," Lauren said.

"That's just the start," Rand said. "Once the indictment is in place, the serious work of doing everything we can to bolster our case really gets started. Even with everything we have, convicting that man is going to take a lot of luck to go along with our hard work."

"What do you think, Marco?" Lauren asked. The DEA agent didn't talk much, but she'd learned he was smart and thoughtful.

"I think we're going to have to get lucky if we want to succeed in bringing down Prentice," he said. "We need to find his weaknesses and target them."

"Does he have any weaknesses?" Sophie asked.

"Lauren was his weakness once," Marco said.

She flushed. When he'd kidnapped her and held her hostage, Prentice said it was to stop her from interfering in his business. But instead of killing her, he'd tried to woo her and persuade her to marry him. "I don't think he feels the same about me now," she said.

"The opposite of love is hate," Marco said. "I still think you matter to him, one way or another."

"Oh, I'd say he definitely hates me now, and

he's playing hardball, getting me fired and making the public think I'm crazy."

"You're not crazy," Marco said. "Just stay smart and be careful. And call me if you need anything."

She turned away, not wanting him to see how his assurance affected her. They'd only spent a few hours together, when he helped rescue her from Prentice, but she'd felt safer with him than she ever had with anyone, despite the fact that, to most people, he was pretty intimidating—hard muscles, hard eyes and an expression that said he was untouched by events around him.

Rand checked his watch. "I hate to break up this party, but we have to go. We've only got an hour for lunch, plus I left Lotte in the Cruiser." Lotte was Rand's police dog, a Belgian Malinois who had helped locate Lauren.

"Give her a biscuit and an ear scratch for me," Lauren said. "And we all have to get back to work, me included. I've got a lawyer to call."

"I won't be long." Sophie hugged her goodbye. "Maybe we'll take in a movie later."

The men left with Sophie, and Abby prepared to take her leave, also. "I think Mr. Tall, Dark and Deadly has a thing for you," she teased as she collected her purse and sunglasses from the kitchen counter.

"Marco?" Lauren's face grew warm. "He was just being nice."

"Marco is never 'just nice,'" Abby said. "Not that he's not a decent guy, but he's very reserved. And a little scary."

"Do you think so?" She'd never felt afraid with Marco.

"He was in Special Forces," Abby said. "Those guys are all a little scary. But very sexy, too." She nudged Lauren. "And I think he definitely likes you. You should ask him out."

"I don't need another rejection right now."

"I don't think he'd reject you," Abby said.

"Even if you're right, now's not the time to start a new relationship. I really need to get my life together."

"Maybe Marco would help." At Lauren's scowl, Abby held up her hands in a defensive gesture. "Okay, okay, I'll stop matchmaking. But, you know—keep it in mind."

The apartment felt emptier than ever when the women were gone. Lauren set about putting away coffee cups and wiping down the counter. After she spoke with Shawn, her lawyer friend, she should update her résumé. And maybe see about doing some freelancing. The local university might need someone in their television department.

She returned to her list and began making

notes. Was there a way to get hold of Richard Prentice's tax records? Maybe through some kind of public records request? That might be revealing...

Pounding on the door made her jump—not a friendly knock, but a heavy beating against the wood that made the wall shake. She grabbed up her phone, ready to hit the speed dial for 9-1-1. "Who is it?" she called in a shaky voice.

"I have a delivery for Lauren Starling."

She tiptoed to the door and peered through the peephole. A burly man in a tracksuit stood on the landing. "You're not with a delivery company," she said. "Go away."

"I have a package for you." He held up a box about eight inches square.

"I don't want it. Go away."

"I'm going to leave it here on the landing. You need to open it."

"Go away before I call the police."

"Suit yourself."

She watched as he set the box on the door-mat and walked away. She waited a full five minutes, heart racing, mind whirling. Who was sending her a package? Was this some kind of joke, or a bomb?

Finally, reasoning there was only one way to learn the answer to her questions, she eased open the door and looked around. The area was deserted. Quickly, she picked up the package and took it inside, where she set it carefully on the table and stared at it.

No return address. No postage or metered label, either. She put her ear to it. No ticking. But would a bomb necessarily tick? She wished Rand and Lotte were still here. The dog could probably tell if the package contained explosives. She could call them, but Rand had enough on his mind right now without worrying about her. The local police might help— or they would just as easily dismiss her as that crazy woman who'd been on television. She couldn't take any more humiliation. Better to handle this herself.

Feeling a little silly, she grabbed a knife and slit open the end of the box. Inside, she glimpsed red foil paper and white silk ribbon. Less afraid now, she worked the knife around until she could lift off the top. Inside the first box was a second, gift-wrapped package. Again, no label.

She carefully worked loose the ribbon on this box and opened the flaps. Inside was a single dried rose and a printed card. "In loving memory," the card read, "of Lauren Montgomery Starling."

Trembling, she turned the card over. Printed

in pencil, in neat block letters, were the words, "Such a short life wasted. We'll all miss you when you're gone."

Chapter Two

Marco stood in line behind Rand and Sophie at the sandwich shop, but his mind was still back at the apartment with Lauren. The first time he'd laid eyes on her in that abandoned mine tunnel where she'd been imprisoned, he'd felt a connection to her. Not just physical attraction—any man might have felt that for the blonde, blue-eyed beauty with the killer figure. The affinity he felt for Lauren went deeper than that, to something in his core. Which was crazy, really. They didn't have anything in common. She was a beauty queen celebrity who lived in the public eye. He'd made a life out of skulking in the shadows.

Maybe it was her strength that resonated with him. It was different from the physical power and mental discipline he practiced, but her ability to endure moved him. She'd had to deal with more trouble in the past few months than most people would ever face in a lifetime, but she still managed to keep smiling and keep fighting. The smile had been a little shakier today; losing her job had to hurt. The stress of all that had happened to her was showing; she was drawn and pale. If Prentice was behind this latest attack on her, Marco wanted to find the guy and teach him a lesson he'd never forget.

His phone buzzed and he slipped it from his pocket and glanced at the screen. Pls come. More trble. Don't say anythng 2 others. Don't want 2 upset Sophie. Lauren.

He pocketed the phone once more and tapped Rand on the shoulder. "I'm going to skip lunch," he said. "Something's come up."

"Anything wrong?"

"Nah. I just remembered something I have to do. Anyway, you know what they say about three being a crowd." He nodded to Sophie. "I'll see you soon."

He sauntered out of the shop—Mr. Smooth, not a care in the world. But every nerve vibrated with worry. Lauren wouldn't have contacted him unless she was in real trouble. Though they'd spent some tense hours together when they were trapped in that old mine on Prentice's estate, he was still a stranger to her. But who else did she have to turn to in the face of real danger? Her sister and her friends couldn't handle a real threat, while he'd spent most of his adult life fighting off enemies of one kind or another.

He reached Lauren's apartment a few minutes later and she opened the door while he was still crossing the parking lot. Clearly, she'd been watching for him. "Thank you for coming," she said. She leaned against the door as if even staying upright was an effort.

He took her arm and guided her back into the apartment, then shut and locked the door behind them. "What is it?" he asked. "What's wrong?"

"A man delivered this a few minutes ago." She led him to the kitchen table, where a brightly wrapped box looked like leftovers from a birthday party. "All that was in it was this dried-up flower and that card."

He bent over the card, not touching it, and read the message printed there. "Look on the back," she said.

He flipped the card over, and clenched his hands into fists. "Someone is trying to frighten you," he said.

"It's working." She studied his face, searching for what—reassurance? Hope?

He could give her neither. "We can check for fingerprints," he said. "But we probably won't find any."

"No, I don't think you will. And I didn't

recognize the man who delivered it, though I wouldn't be surprised to find out he works for Prentice."

"Why do you say that?" he asked.

"He was the type of guy Richard uses for his private security force—beefy and menacing. Guys who get off on being intimidating." She shuddered, and he fought the urge to put his arms around her, to comfort her. She'd mentioned before that Prentice's guards had tried to bully and take advantage of her, pawing at her when they thought they could get away with it. The idea made him see red. If he ever got one of those guys alone…

Not a productive thought. He needed to focus on the task at hand. They both stared at the small card—a harmless piece of paper that carried such a potent threat. "Is this his way of saying he's going to kill me?" she asked.

"Maybe." No sense sugarcoating the truth. If she was dead, she'd stop agitating for Prentice's arrest. The billionaire had killed before to silence his enemies. Marco was sure of that, even if the task force had never been able to find conclusive evidence to link him to the killings. "You need to show this to the police."

"And tell them what?" Anger flared, the sharp edge in her voice a good sign, he thought. She wasn't going to sink into despair. "Do I say

Richard Prentice is threatening me? He'll deny it and issue another statement about how obsessed I am with him and how crazy I am. And they'll believe him, because everyone knows you can't trust an unstable person like me."

He gripped her shoulders, not hurting her, but demanding her attention. "Don't let what people say come true," he said. "You're not crazy or unstable. You're strong. You were strong enough to get away from Prentice the first time. We can outsmart him now."

"We?"

"I'm sticking with you until I'm sure you're safe."

"So you think this is a real threat?" The last word was barely a whisper.

"Yes. And you're right—the police aren't the answer. Going to them is probably exactly what Prentice expects you to do, what he wants, even." He led her to the sofa and sat with her. "As long as he can keep this in the press, he can keep hammering home the idea that you've lost it. By ignoring him, we frustrate him and force his hand."

"But what will he do next?"

"I don't know. But it's why I can't leave you alone."

She laughed, but with no mirth. That was the sound of someone fighting to maintain control.

"This is ridiculous. You're not my personal bodyguard. And you have a job. You have to work."

"You're the chief witness in the case we're building against Prentice," he said. "The captain will agree we need to keep you safe."

"Haven't you been paying attention? You don't have a case. Prentice is doing his best to paint me as the crazy woman who can't be trusted. Anything I say against him is obviously a figment of my troubled mind."

"That's what he wants people to think, but we know it's not true. And other people know it, too. You have to stay strong and not let this get to you."

"Did they train you to give these pep talks when you were in Special Forces? Because it's not working."

"There goes my career as a motivational speaker."

His attempt at humor didn't move her. "Why is he doing this now?" she asked. "It's been almost a month since I escaped his ranch."

"He was hiding out on some Caribbean island, working to get the charges against him dropped and probably hoping you'd go away. You haven't, so he's decided to turn up the heat. You know enough about him that you're still a real threat to him."

"Or maybe I'm a loose end he wants tied up," she said.

"Or maybe he wants revenge because you turned down his advances," he said. "Love can make people do crazy things."

"Oh, please! Richard Prentice doesn't love anyone but himself."

"Maybe *love* isn't the right word… He was obsessed with you, and I don't think people like him turn those feelings off like a light switch. The obsession just…transforms. Turns darker."

"Thanks. Now you're really creeping me out." She rubbed her hands up and down her arms as if warding off a chill. "So what are we going to do? You can't babysit me twenty-four hours a day."

He stood and began to pace, studying the apartment. It was a ground-floor unit in a complex that faced a side street off the main highway. The front door opened onto a large parking lot, and there were large windows on all sides. No security. No guards. Easy in-and-out access. "Anyone could break in here with no trouble at all," he said. "We need to move you to a safer location."

"I can't afford to move. I'm unemployed, remember?"

"You can't afford to stay here, either."

"Do you really think it's that bad?" she

asked. "I mean, would he really kill me? Isn't convincing everyone I'm crazy enough?"

"We don't have the proof we need, but we believe he's had people killed before," Marco said. "There was his pilot—and don't forget that fish seller, Alan Milbanks."

She nodded. "Milbanks's death meant the chief source for my story about Richard Prentice was out of the picture. Very convenient."

"Not having you around would be convenient for him, too. Do you want to take that chance?"

"No." She straightened and lifted her chin, determined. "Do the Rangers have a safe house or something?"

"No. You can come to my place."

"Your place?" She choked back a laugh.

"What's so funny?"

"You live in a duplex. With Rand in the other half."

"Exactly. You'll have twice the protection. And your sister's over at his place all the time anyway."

"No, Marco, I can't. What will people think?" She flushed. "I mean, if your place is like Rand's, there's only one bedroom."

He liked it when she blushed that way—it did something to his insides that he didn't want to think about too much. He'd rather enjoy the feeling. "I'll sleep on the sofa."

"I couldn't."

"Go." He put a hand to her back and urged her toward her bedroom. "Pack a bag. I know what I'm doing." His duplex wasn't ideal, but it was off the beaten path, had only one street leading in and out, bars on the windows and a reinforced door. And it wouldn't be the first place anyone would look for her. Keeping her there would buy him more time to identify any real threat.

"If anyone but you tried to order me around like this, I'd tell them exactly what they could do with their bossy attitude," she said as she headed down the short hallway off the living room. "But you make me believe you really *do* know what you're doing."

While he waited, he scanned the parking lot in front of the apartment. He focused on a big guy across the street. The man wore a blue-and-white tracksuit and had a pair of binoculars trained on Lauren's front windows. Marco moved closer to the window and raised the blinds. The big guy didn't move. Marco glared. No reaction from the guy in the tracksuit. He might have been a mannequin, except they didn't make mannequins that burly, and after a few seconds, the watcher reached up to scratch his ear.

Marco moved quickly down the hall to Lauren's bedroom and stopped in the doorway, stunned at the sight of her up to her elbows in lace and satin. She'd apparently dumped the contents of her dresser drawers on the bed and was sorting through the pile of panties, bras, stockings, negligees and who knew what other items of feminine apparel.

She glanced over her shoulder at him. "It was easier to just dump everything and sort through them this way." She grabbed up a handful of items and danced over to an open suitcase in the dresser and dropped them inside, then spent some time arranging them, smoothing them out and humming to herself.

"There's a man standing out front, watching your apartment," Marco said. "He's not even trying to hide it. He has this huge pair of binoculars, like a bird-watcher would use."

"Maybe he is a bird-watcher." She giggled, a high-pitched, unnatural sound.

"Come look and tell me if you know him."

"All right."

She glided down the hall ahead of him, still humming, and went to the window. "Oh, yes, I know him." She waved like someone greeting a friend at the airport.

"How do you know him?" Marco asked.

"He delivered that package." She waved idly toward the box on the table.

"All right. Go ahead and finish packing. We should leave soon."

"Yes, I'll do that. I have a gorgeous new dress. I was in the mall yesterday and saw it and just had to have it. I'll take it in case we go someplace nice."

Marco frowned. "Are you feeling all right?" he asked.

Her smile didn't waver, though to him it seemed forced. "Why wouldn't I be feeling all right?"

"You've been under a lot of stress." He spoke carefully, watching her eyes. Her gaze shifted around the room, as if frantically searching for something. "Most people would be anxious in a situation like this."

"Yes. I am anxious." She twisted her hands together. "I just… I'd love to go for a run now. Burn off some of this extra energy." She turned to a dresser and began pulling out exercise tops and shorts, adding them to the pile of clothing on the bed.

Now was not the time for a run. He had to get her away from here, away from the guy in the parking lot, to some place safer. "Would you like me to call Sophie?"

"No! No, don't call Sophie! She's always so worried, worried I'm going to go off the deep end or do something stupid. Something… crazy." She whispered the last word, standing still with a tank top dangling from one hand.

"You're not crazy." He kept his voice calm in the face of the agitation rolling off her in waves. After he'd met her, after he carried her in his arms out of the collapsed mine on Richard Prentice's estate, he'd gone online and done some reading on bipolar disorder. He'd learned that stress and even variations in routine could trigger a manic episode. Lauren's life had been nothing but stress these past months, and she had no more routine—no job or real home or any certainty about the future.

"Maybe…maybe I should call my doctor." She looked at the clothes piled on the bed and the open suitcase. "I took my medication," she said softly. "I always do, even though, sometimes, I don't like the way it makes me feel."

"Maybe the medication just needs…adjusting."

She nodded. "Right. I…I'll call him."

He waited in the bedroom while she went into the living room. He wondered if he should remove the clothes from the bed—pack for her. But no. That was too personal. Too patronizing, even.

He backed out of the room and rejoined her as she was hanging up the phone. "I talked to the nurse," she said. "She suggested I take more of one of my pills, and she's calling in another prescription I can take if I need to."

He nodded. "Do you need anything from me? Help with packing? Something to eat?"

"No, I'm good. I'll just, uh, finish up back here."

"I'll keep an eye on our friend."

"Friend?"

He nodded toward the parking lot. "The bird-watcher."

She laughed again, and the sound continued all the way down the hall. The sound worried him a little, but it also made him angry. Why did such a beautiful, vibrant woman have to be plagued with emotions that veered so easily out of control? Why was she at the mercy of a disease she hadn't asked for and didn't want? He'd spent his life fighting off physical enemies, first in a street gang, then the military, now as a law enforcement officer. But what could he do to help her?

THE MEDICATION BEGAN to work quickly, a numbing fog slipping over the anxiety and agitation that were the first signs of a climb toward mania. Lauren hated this lethargy and *not feeling* as much as she dreaded the extreme highs or lows of her disease. Why couldn't she just be normal?

She finished packing her suitcase, stuffing in clothes without care, putting off having to go back into the living room and face Marco. This hadn't been a bad episode. She hadn't burst into song or taken off her clothes or made a pass at him—all things she'd done before her diagnosis had provided an explanation for her bizarre behavior. But she'd waved her underwear around in front of him, and laughed at the idea of a man stalking her.

He was so solemn and unemotional. What must he think of a woman who, even on her best days, tended to feel things too deeply?

In the end, she didn't have to go to him; he came to her. "Are you ready to go?" he asked. "We can stop and get some lunch on the way."

"Sure." She zipped the suitcase closed and looked at the disarray of the room.

"It's all right," he said. "You can clean this up later." He picked up the suitcase. "Do you have everything you need?"

"Yes." She grabbed the two pill bottles from the top of the dresser and cradled them to her chest. "I'm ready."

She put the pill bottles in her purse and followed him to the door. Sophie had rented the apartment when she'd decided to relocate to Montrose to be with Rand, and Lauren only stayed there because she had no place else to go. She couldn't claim to be attached to the place, but still, it felt bad to be leaving so soon, to face more uncertainty.

Deep breath. Center. She closed her eyes and inhaled through her nose, the way the therapist at the psychiatric hospital had shown her. She could deal with this.

When she opened her eyes, Marco was watching her. She saw no judgment in his calm brown eyes. "Are you ready?" he asked.

She nodded. "Is the bird-watcher still out there?"

"He left a few minutes ago. I guess he'd done his job."

"What was his job, do you think? Besides delivering the package."

"He was sending the message that you were being watched. His job was to intimidate you."

"The note did that."

"I guess Prentice likes to cover all the bases."

"What about the package?" She looked around for the creepy gift. "I don't want Sophie finding it when she comes back."

"I've got it." He indicated the shopping bag he must have found in the pantry. "I'll have someone check it out. Maybe we'll get lucky and learn something useful. Come on." He opened the front door and started across the lot, toward the black-and-white FJ Cruiser he'd parked closest to her apartment.

"I'll follow you in my car," she said.

His frown told her he didn't think much of that idea. "You should ride with me."

"I can't just leave my car. I can't be stuck way out at your duplex with no transportation." The idea ramped up her anxiety again, like something clawing at the back of her throat.

"Then, we'll take your car and I'll send someone back later for mine."

"All right." Relief made her weak. When they reached the car she hesitated, then handed him the keys. "You'd better drive. Sometimes the pills make me sleepy."

He nodded and unlocked the trunk and stowed her suitcase and the shopping bag, then climbed into the driver's seat. "What pharmacy do you use?"

Her prescription was ready. Once they'd collected it, he swung by a sandwich shop for lunch. She wasn't hungry—another side effect of the medication—but she ordered to avoid explaining this to him. Finally they were on the highway headed to his place. She put her head back against the headrest and closed her eyes. Maybe when they got to his place she'd take a nap. But she'd need to unpack, and she still had to call her lawyer, Shawn…

"Have you had any trouble with your car lately?"

She opened her eyes and sat up straight. "No. What kind of trouble?"

"The brakes." He pumped the brake pedal, but the car only sped up, down a long incline that curved sharply at the bottom.

"What's wrong with the brakes?" She leaned over to study the speedometer, the needle creeping up past seventy miles an hour. "Why are we going so fast?"

"I think someone may have tampered with your car." His voice remained calm, but the fine lines around his eyes deepened, and his knuckles on the steering wheel were white with strain.

She covered her mouth with her hand and stared at the highway hurtling toward them with ever-increasing speed. At the bottom of the hill was a curve, and beyond the curve, a deep canyon. If their car went over the edge, they would never survive.

Chapter Three

Marco didn't look at Lauren, but he could hear the sudden, sharp intake of her breath and sense her fear like a third presence in the car. He tried pumping the brake pedal, but nothing happened. He pressed it to the floor and downshifted to first gear. The engine whined in protest, and the car slowed, but not enough.

"Hang on," he said, raising his voice over the whine of the protesting engine. He pulled back on the lever for the emergency brake and the car began to fishtail wildly. He strained to keep hold of the wheel. Lauren whimpered, but said nothing.

They were well out of town now, empty public land and private ranches stretching for miles on either side, with no houses or businesses or people to see their distress and report it. Not that anyone could do anything to help them anyway. If they had any chance of surviving a crash, he had to try to regain control of the car.

They continued to accelerate, racing toward the curve at the bottom of the hill. He steered toward the side of the road, gravel flying as the back wheels slid onto the shoulder. The idea was to let friction slow the car more, but the dropoff past the shoulder was too steep; if he kept going he'd roll the car.

Back on the roadway, the car continued to skid and sway like a drunken frat boy. The smell of burning rubber and exhaust stung his nose and eyes. If they blew a tire, he'd lose control completely; the car might roll. He released the emergency brake and grabbed the steering wheel with both hands. "Brace yourself against the dash and lean toward me!" he commanded.

She didn't argue. As she skewed her body toward his seat, he could smell her perfume, sweet and floral, overlaying the sharp, metallic scent of fear. He wanted to tell her everything would be all right, that she didn't have to worry. But he couldn't lie like that.

He came at the guardrail sideways, sparks flying as the bumper scraped the metal rails, gravel popping beneath the tires. The scream of metal on metal filled the air, making him want to cover his ears, but of course he couldn't. He kept hold of the wheel, guiding the car along the guardrail.

Friction and a gentler slope combined to slow them, and as the guardrail ended, he was able to use the emergency brake to bring them to a halt on the side of the road. He shut off the engine and neither of them spoke, the only sounds the tick of the cooling motor and their own heavy breathing.

He had to pry his hands off the steering wheel and force himself to look at her. "Are you all right?" he asked.

She nodded, and pushed the hair back from her face with shaking hands. "My car isn't, though. What happened?"

"The brakes failed."

"I had the car serviced before I came out here," she said. "My mechanic said it was fine."

"It sat at that overlook in the park for a few days, and then at the wrecking yard for a few weeks. An animal—a rabbit or something— could have chewed the brake cable." He didn't really think that was what had happened, but he didn't want to frighten her.

"But I've been driving the car for weeks now and it's been fine." She turned even paler. "What if this had happened when I was alone?"

What, indeed? He unfastened his seat belt. "I'm going to take a look."

He had to wrench the hood open, past the broken headlight and bent bumper. He fixed the prop in place and stared down into the tangle of hoses and wires. After a moment, she joined him.

"I couldn't open my door, so I crawled over the console," she said. "Can you tell what went wrong?"

He leaned under the hood and popped the top over the master cylinder reservoir. It was completely dry, only a thin coating of brake fluid left behind. That explained why the brakes had failed, but why had the fluid drained?

He walked around to the side of the car and knelt beside the front tire. He reached over the tire and grasped the flexible hose that led to the brakes. It felt intact, but as he ran his finger along the hose, he found a moon-shaped slit—the kind of damage that could be made by someone reaching over the tire and stabbing the brake hose with a knife.

"What is it?" she asked, following him around to the other side of the car.

He knelt and checked that hose. "Someone punctured the brake line on both sides," he said. "The brake fluid drained out, and that caused the brakes to fail."

She steadied herself with one hand on the fender of the car. "The bird-watcher?"

"Maybe. Or it could have been done while we were at lunch." Big failure on his part. He should have taken the physical threat to her more seriously.

"The parking lot at my apartment has a surveillance camera," she said. "I mean, don't they all, these days?"

"Maybe, but a lot of places use dummy cameras that don't really film anything." He'd bet her apartment complex fell into that category. "And whoever did this is probably smart enough to avoid any cameras."

"We should call the police," she said.

He glanced around them, getting his bearings. Drying rabbit brush covered an open expanse of prairie, only the occasionally stunted piñon providing shade. Here and there purple aster offered a surprising blot of color against an otherwise brown landscape. "This is the edge of national park land," he said.

"Ranger territory." She completed the idea for him and managed a weak smile. "Well, that's something. I wasn't looking forward to talking to the police."

He pulled out his phone. "I'll call someone to give us a ride, then get a wrecker to haul the car to headquarters where we can take a closer look at it."

Her hand on his wrist stopped him. He looked down at the slender, white fingers, nails perfectly shaped and painted a soft pink. "Before anyone else gets here, I just wanted to say thank you," she said. "You saved my life—again."

He covered her hand briefly with his own. "It's going to be okay," he said. "Everything that happens brings us one step closer to stopping Prentice."

"Thank you, too, for not freaking out about my illness," she said. "I'm getting better at working at controlling it, but sometimes…"

"I know. It's okay."

Her head snapped up, her gaze searching. "How do you know?"

"I did some reading." He shrugged. "I like to understand what's going on around me."

"There's nothing understandable about this disease."

"No, but you're doing great. A lot of people would crack under the stress you've been under, but you're hanging in there. You're tough."

"Yeah, I'm tough as a marshmallow." She moved her hand away and squared her shoulders. "But I won't let that stop me. And I won't let Richard Prentice stop me. Maybe he's done me a favor, getting me fired from the station. Now going after him is going to be my job."

"I'm already on it," he said.

"Then, with both of us on his case, he doesn't stand a chance."

LAUREN WISHED SHE was as confident as Marco sounded. She'd meant what she'd said about making convicting Richard Prentice her full-time job. She desperately needed the focus on work to quell her anxiety and tamp down the threatening mania, but the idea that the man she was investigating wanted her dead shook her to the core.

All she wanted was a normal life—a job and a husband and maybe a family one day. But all those things seemed so out of reach. Her own brain had betrayed her, and while the doctors and therapists had assured her that she could live a normal, productive life with bipolar disorder, she suspected them of lying to make her feel better. Or was that just the depressive side of her disorder pulling her down? She couldn't even trust her own thoughts these days.

While Marco contacted Ranger headquarters and summoned a wrecker, she walked around to the other side of the car and phoned Sophie. "Hey, I was just on my way back to the apartment," Sophie said when the call connected. "I thought maybe we could take in a movie or something."

"I'm not there."

"Where are you?"

"With Marco. My car broke down and we're headed over to Ranger headquarters."

"What happened? What's wrong with the car?"

"Marco thinks someone sabotaged the brakes. We're okay," she hastened to add. "The car's kind of beat up, but we're fine."

"Was Marco with you when it happened?" Sophie asked.

"Yes. I'm going to stay with him a few days."

"With Marco?" Sophie's surprise was clear.

"He thinks it will be safer. There was someone watching our apartment earlier." She didn't tell Sophie about the package with its implied death threat. Thank goodness Marco had taken it with them. She didn't want to upset her sister, but also talking about the note made it too real.

"I'm sure it is safer." Sophie sounded amused. "That should be interesting. I think he's attracted to you."

She shifted her gaze to Marco. Did all her friends think that he was interested in her? Then, why couldn't she see it? He stood with his back to her, giving her a great view of his broad shoulders, muscular arms, narrow waist and admittedly perfect backside. He looked like the after photo in the advertisement for a workout program. Physically fit and totally together. The perfect match for a basket case like her—not. "He wants to get Prentice," she said. "I'm the quickest route to that goal. It's nothing personal."

"I don't know about that. He's good at hiding his feelings, but he's bound to have some, somewhere beneath that stoic facade."

"You should consider staying with Rand," Lauren said. "At least for a few days." She didn't want someone coming to the apartment looking for her and finding Sophie there alone.

"Not a bad idea," Sophie said.

"Make him go back to the apartment with you to get your things," Lauren said.

"Do you really think it's that dangerous?"

She glanced at her destroyed car, the paint scraped from the side in a jagged, violent wound. "Yes," she said simply.

Marco tucked his phone back into his pocket and turned toward Lauren. "I have to go," she said. The last thing she wanted was for him to overhear Sophie's analysis of his potential as a love interest. "I'll call you later."

"Someone will be here to pick us up in a few minutes," Marco said once she'd hung up. "Everything okay?"

"Yes. I was just letting Sophie know what was happening."

"Good idea." He leaned back against the car and scanned the horizon. He had a stillness about him she envied, as if whenever he wanted he could quiet all the busyness and distraction that plagued her.

"What are you thinking?" she asked.

"That it would be hard for a sniper to position himself here. The country's too open."

Her knees went weak, and she joined him in leaning against the car. "You think someone might be out there, ready to shoot us?"

He shook his head. "It's not a good location."

She closed her eyes. This was too real. Someone—probably Richard Prentice—wanted her dead.

"I'll feel better when we get out of the open," he said. "Someone will probably come along soon to see if we crashed—to make sure we're dead."

She swallowed hard. "Can we talk about something else, please?"

He didn't take his gaze from the horizon. "What do you want to talk about?"

"Do you have any brothers or sisters?"

"I had six older sisters."

"Big family." She envied him. Sophie was the only family she had. "Do you see them often?"

"Not really. They live in California." He fell

silent for a moment, then added, "Only four of them are still alive."

"Oh. I'm sorry."

"One sister died of an overdose. The other disappeared. We don't know what happened to her."

And here she'd thought she was the only one with troubles. "That must be hard," she said. Not the innocuous conversation she'd hoped for.

"It is what it is." He straightened. "Here's our ride."

A Cruiser identical to the one Marco usually drove made a U-turn and pulled in behind Lauren's disabled car. Montrose County sheriff's deputy Lance Carpenter, the local representative on the task force, left the vehicle running as he stepped out of the driver's seat and pushed his Stetson back on his head. "Trying out for the demolition derby?" he asked.

"Very funny." Marco shoved the car keys into Lance's hands. "Give these to the wrecker driver—and make sure nobody touches anything around the brakes until the techs have gone over it." He took Lauren's hand and pulled her toward the Cruiser.

"Where do you think you're going?" Lance asked.

"I need to get Lauren out of here before

whoever cut those brake lines shows up to admire the results of his handiwork."

"What am I supposed to do?" Lance asked.

"Wait here for the wrecker driver."

"Should we have left him?" Lauren asked as Marco gunned the engine and they headed toward the park.

"The wrecker will be there any minute now, and I wasn't comfortable with you standing around out in the open."

"The idea that I have a target on my back doesn't seem real to me."

"The trick is to balance the awareness of danger with the need to keep from panicking." He glanced at her. "Not easy, I know."

"I think I'm glad I got the extra meds."

"I want to stop by headquarters and talk to the captain, then we'll get you settled at my place."

"I left my bag in the car."

"Lance will bring it."

"You seem pretty sure of that. Do you Rangers communicate via ESP or secret code or something?"

"He's got my back." He glanced at her. "Now you're with me, so he's got your back, too."

His words—and the certainty with which he spoke them, sent a different kind of heat curling through her—part old-fashioned lust and part the unfamiliar warmth of acceptance. Her disease had separated her from others for so long. How ironic that a threat to her life had involved her with a community of friends again.

Half a dozen Cruisers filled the spaces in front of the task force headquarters building. "Something's up." Marco parked along the side of the road and was out of the vehicle before Lauren had even unbuckled her seat belt.

She hurried after him, running to keep up. Inside the building, uniformed officers crowded the small, low-ceilinged rooms. "What's going on?" Marco asked.

"You'll find out as soon as everyone's here."

The captain retreated to his office, shutting the door behind him.

"Any idea what this is about?" Lieutenant Michael Dance, Abby's boyfriend, asked.

Everyone shook their heads. "All I know is, the captain has been on the phone most of the morning," Carmen Redhorse, an officer with the Colorado Bureau of Investigations, said. "Whatever this is about, he's not happy."

Twenty minutes later, Graham finally emerged from his office and surveyed the room full of officers. "Where's Lance?"

"I'm here." Lauren looked over her shoulder to see the deputy in the doorway. He made his way over to them and handed Lauren her overnight bag, then gave Marco a slip of paper. "The car's on its way to the impound lot."

"Did you take a look at the brake lines?" Marco asked.

"Yeah. They look cut to me, but we'll know more when the techs are done."

"If I could have your attention." Graham stood at the front of the room and held up one hand. A hush settled over the crowd. Lauren clenched her hands into fists and fought to keep still; the tension was contagious.

The captain cleared his throat. "The grand jury has failed to indict Richard Prentice of any of the charges against him," he said.

Chapter Four

Lauren blinked, sure she had heard the captain wrong. He must mean the grand jury had indicted Richard Prentice, right? She turned to Marco, his face the stone mask of an Aztec warrior. "What's happening?" she asked.

"Somehow, Prentice managed to get off," he said.

"I don't understand," she said, still dazed. "He kidnapped me. He held me prisoner. You saw where he was keeping me."

"We saw." Rand's expression was as grim as everyone else's. Even Lotte, who stood by his side, looked upset. "We know you're telling the truth, not just about the kidnapping, but about the other crimes he's involved in."

"At least you believe me," Lauren said. "The jury obviously didn't. They believed Richard when he said I was making everything up."

"Maybe it wasn't you," Marco said. "Maybe it was something else."

"They didn't believe me because they think I'm crazy," she said. "I'm mentally ill, so of course I must be a liar, too. I made the whole thing up. It was a wild fantasy I concocted just to get attention." Online columnists and bloggers had already wasted plenty of bandwidth speculating on the reasons for Lauren's "obsession" with the billionaire. Because of course, why would he ever be obsessed with her? Sure, she was pretty, they said. But she had a history of wild behavior. So of course, her side of the story couldn't be trusted.

"Prentice is trying to distract people by making this case about you," Marco said. "It's a game he's playing, but it's a game he isn't going to win."

"What will you do?" she asked.

"We'll have to start over." Captain Ellison joined them. "We're going to work the case as if it's brand-new, reexamining every lead, taking a second look at every bit of evidence. I want everyone focused on this. It's going to take a lot of long days and hard work, but we'll build a case the prosecution can't deny."

Around her, heads lifted and shoulders straightened. The anger they'd felt moments earlier transformed into determination to see justice done. Lauren wished their energy was contagious, but she was still reeling from the knowledge that what had happened to her had been so easily dismissed by the twenty-three members of the grand jury. She touched Marco's arm. "I'll go now and let you get to work."

"Let me go with you," he said. He pulled keys from his pocket.

"No, you're needed here." She looked around the room. Already, members of the task force were pulling out files and booting up computers, ready to get to work.

"It's not safe for you to be alone," Marco said.

"I'll be fine. I'll call Sophie to come pick me up." It wasn't as if she could drive her wrecked car. "Now that he's swayed the grand jury, Prentice knows I'm no threat."

He was going to argue with her, she could tell, but the door burst open and Emma stalked in, the heels of her stilettos striking the tile floor so hard Lauren expected to see sparks. Jaw clenched, eyes blazing, she looked ready to punch someone. "Hello, Emma," Graham said, as calm as ever. "I take it you heard the news about Richard Prentice."

Emma set her bag down on the edge of a desk. "Officially, I'm here to get your statement on this turn of events for my story," she said. "Unofficially, I need to vent to someone who understands my frustration. How could they do this? How could they ignore all the evidence you had against him?"

"We'll never know for sure, but I'm guessing they interpreted everything as circumstantial," Graham said. "We don't have fingerprints, tape recordings or any written records, and only one eyewitness."

"Whom they don't consider reliable," Lauren said. She blocked any protests they might have made. "Don't deny it. I'm not."

"He is doing a smear campaign against you," Emma said. "My editor sent me a copy of the press release Prentice issued this afternoon."

"What does it say?" Michael asked.

She leaned against the desk and pulled up the press release on her phone. "There's a bunch of malarkey about justice being done, proves his innocence, blah, blah, blah." She waved her hand. "But here's the part about Lauren. 'It is painful to know my friend Lauren Starling is so ill. I can find no other explanation for why she would attack the one man who truly tried to help her. I hope she will find the help she needs to get well. On her behalf I am making a generous donation toward mental health research.'" She made a face. "Excuse me while I vomit. The man is disgusting."

Everyone gathered around Emma to examine the press release and rehash the grand jury's ruling. Lauren took the opportunity to slip outside, where she texted Sophie to pick her up at Ranger headquarters.

She slipped the phone back into her purse and walked over to the gazebo at the far end of the parking lot, which offered a view of the canyon that gave the park its name. The Black Canyon of the Gunnison plunged more than twenty-five hundred feet down to the Gunnison River. Sun penetrated the bottom for only a few hours each day, giving the canyon its name. The land around the gorge shimmered in the early August sun, wind rustling the silvery leaves of sage and rattling the dry cones of stunted piñons.

When Lauren had first arrived here over two months ago the harsh landscape had repelled, even frightened her. She saw nothing beautiful in dry grasses and empty land. The quiet and emptiness of this place made her feel too small and alone.

But her weeks of captivity had changed her opinion of this place. With nothing to do in the early days of her stay at Prentice's mansion—before he moved her into the abandoned mine—she'd spent hours staring out at the prairie. She'd learned to appreciate the stillness of the land, which had called forth a similar stillness within her. She began to see beauty in the thousand shades of green and brown in the grasses and trees. Now the emptiness that had once repelled her calmed her.

The squeal of brakes announced the arrival of a car. Lauren turned to see Sophie's blue sedan pulling into the lot. She hurried to her sister and slid into the passenger seat.

"I can't believe it," Sophie said before Lauren could speak. "Rand just called and told me Richard Prentice is getting off scot-free."

"I guess so." Lauren buckled her seat belt and leaned back against the headrest.

"What are we going to do?" Sophie asked.

Lauren closed her eyes. She was so tired. "Right now, I just want to go home," she said.

Sophie put the car in gear and backed out of the lot. "Is something wrong?" she asked after a moment. "Are you not feeling well?"

"I'm okay. I took an extra pill and it's making me a little sleepy." She hoped that was all it was. Sometimes lethargy was a sign of depression.

"Why did you take an extra pill? Should you be doing that?" Sophie's voice rose in alarm.

Lauren opened her eyes. "It's okay. That's what the doctor said to do."

"You talked to your doctor? Why?"

She knew better than to ignore the question. Sophie wouldn't let it go. She'd always been like that, never giving in on anything. Lauren should be grateful; Sophie's refusal to give up on her had led to her coming to Montrose and prodding the Rangers into finding her.

"I had a minor manic episode this morning. Nothing big, and it's under control now."

"When was this? What happened?"

"After you and Emma left. After Abby left, too. I think it was just the stress of finding out about my job." Though her life had been nothing but stress for months now.

"What happened?"

"Nothing. I just got a little…giddy. Feeling out of control. Marco was there, and he helped calm me down."

"Marco was there?"

"I called him when I realized someone was watching the apartment."

"That must be why he left the café in such a hurry," Sophie said. "Who was the watcher?"

"I don't know. Marco didn't know him, either, and the man left. But there was something else—something I didn't tell you before."

"What's that?" Sophie kept her eyes on the road, her expression calm.

"The guy who was watching delivered a package. Like a gift box, but all it had in it was a dried-up flower and a note."

"What did the note say?"

"It was like one of those memorial cards you sometimes see at funerals, with the words *in memory of* written on it. It had my name on it." She shuddered at the memory. "The Rangers are going to look into it, but I doubt they'll find anything. Someone was trying to scare me."

Sophie didn't say anything for a long while, taking it in. Lauren closed her eyes again.

"I'm glad Marco was with you," Sophie said. "The guy doesn't say much, but he's deep. And any bad guy would think twice before tangling with him."

That was true enough. Beyond his physical strength, Marco had perfected an intimidating attitude. Which made his gentleness with her all the more touching.

"Hey, I thought you were going to stay with him," Sophie said.

"I was, but we've had a change of plans. He needs to devote himself to the investigation. And now that Richard has gotten the charges against him dropped, I'm no longer a threat."

"Aren't you?" Sophie asked. "You aren't going to give up because of one grand jury's mistakes, are you?"

"I don't know." She was just so tired—of always fighting, of having to be strong when she felt so weak.

"You can't give up," Sophie said. "Giving up

means he wins—that the lies he's told about you are true."

She opened her eyes again and forced herself to sit up straight and look at her sister. "Then, what do we do?"

"We do what we can to help with the investigation," Sophie said. "We talk to people, find out what they know."

"Who do we talk to?" Her one contact on the case, Alan Milbanks, was dead.

"Why don't we start with Phil? We'll find out if Prentice paid him to tell the press those lies about you."

The last person Lauren wanted to see was her ex-husband, but Sophie's reasoning made sense. Talking to Phil was a smart and relatively safe place to start. "All right," she said. "We'll talk to him."

"Do you know where he's staying?"

She took out her phone and scrolled through her list of contacts until she found the address of the rehab facility in Grand Junction where Phil was staying. She read it off to Sophie.

"Great. We can be there in an hour." She punched the address into her GPS. "Why don't you take a nap while I drive? I'll wake you when we get there."

Lauren closed her eyes again and tried to get more comfortable in her seat. If only she'd wake up from her nap to find the past few months had been nothing but a nightmare—not the awful reality she had to keep surviving.

LATER THAT AFTERNOON Marco trained the high-powered binoculars on Richard Prentice's mansion. The gray stone castle, complete with crenellated towers and a fake drawbridge, was the billionaire's way of giving the finger to the county officials who had thwarted his plans to sell the park in-holding to them at inflated prices. The castle blocked a park visitor's best view of the Curecanti Needle, a famous rock formation. Now, instead of marveling at the beauty of nature, visitors standing at the Pioneer Point overlook in the park saw this monstrosity.

"See anything?" Rand asked, crouched next to Marco on a rocky outcropping of land just across the boundary line from Prentice's ranch.

"Nope." He swung the binoculars to the left and focused on two muscular men in desert camo, who lounged against a tricked-out black Jeep. One of the men had an AR-15 casually slung over one shoulder. "The troops are taking it easy," Marco said.

Rand grunted. "Their boss is probably feeling pretty secure since the grand jury let him off the hook."

"Something tells me insecurity isn't one of Prentice's problems, ever." He shifted the binoculars farther to the left, to the pile of rubble that marked the entrance to the mine where Lauren had been held. No telling what other illegal booty had been stored in the maze of tunnels. Prentice had been worried enough to order his men to set off explosives and collapse the mine, almost trapping Lauren and her rescuers inside.

Rand must have been thinking about that night, too. "Why didn't the grand jury believe Lauren when she told them what he'd done to her?" he asked.

"People are afraid of mental illness. Prentice and his experts played on that fear."

"What about you?"

Marco lowered the binoculars and stared at his friend. "Are you asking if I'm afraid of Lauren?"

"Not afraid, but do you worry about getting involved with someone who's dealing with something like this?"

He shifted his backpack from his shoulder and stowed the binoculars. "I don't lose sleep worrying about it."

"Sophie told me you volunteered to be her bodyguard. I thought maybe it was because you were interested in her. You know, romantically."

Marco zipped up the pack and shrugged back into it. "She needs protecting. I can protect her. That's all." That was all there could ever be between him and Lauren Starling.

"So you're just above all those messy emotions the rest of us mortals have to deal with," Rand said.

"I don't have time for them." Those "messy emotions" brought complications and distractions he didn't want or need. He turned back to the view of Prentice's castle. "We have a job to do."

Rand stiffened and put a hand on the pistol at his side. "What's that noise?"

The low whine, like the humming of a large mosquito, grew louder. Marco looked around, then up, and spotted what at first looked like a toy plane or one of those radio-controlled aircraft hobbyists flew. "I think it's a drone," he said as the craft hovered over them.

Rand scowled at the intruder. "Is it armed?"

"No, but I think it's spotted us."

"The captain said Prentice had one of these. What do you think it's doing?"

Marco trained the binoculars on the craft. "It looks as if there's a camera attached to the underside, so I'd say it's taking pictures."

"Pictures of what?"

"Of us. Evidence that we're harassing the poor little rich guy."

"Nothing wrong with being rich." Rand gave a big, cheesy smile and waved up at the drone.

Marco lowered the binoculars, resisting the urge to make an obscene gesture at the camera. "No, but there's a lot wrong with being a jerk." And a jerk who used a beautiful, vulnerable woman in his sick games had to be stopped.

Chapter Five

The low-slung cedar and stone buildings of the Dayspring Wellness Center looked more like an exclusive vacation resort than a medical facility. Fountains and flowers dotted the lavish landscaping, and the few people Lauren and Sophie saw once they'd left their car in the parking lot were tanned and casually dressed as if on their way to a tennis game or setting out to hike in the nearby hills.

"Maybe we should look into checking in here," Sophie said as they made their way up a paved walkway lined with brilliant blooming flowers. "This is way nicer than our apartment. And we wouldn't have to cook or clean."

Lauren stopped before a signpost with markers pointing toward the dining room, gym, pool and treatment rooms. "This all must cost a fortune."

"Then, how is Phil paying for it? Wasn't he hassling you for money before you disappeared?"

"He wanted me to increase his support payments." Because Lauren had earned more money than Phil, an actor with a small theater company, the court had ordered her to pay him support after their divorce. "But I haven't given him any money in months." While Prentice had held her captive, she hadn't had access to her bank accounts, then she hadn't been working, recovering from her ordeal. Now that she'd been fired, no telling when she'd be able to pay him.

Then again, not having access to her money had forced him to admit that his drug habit had gotten out of hand, and he had to seek help. When the Rangers had questioned him about her disappearance, he'd been living in a fleabag motel on the edge of town. "Maybe his girlfriend came into money." When they'd divorced, Phil had been seeing an actress he worked with.

"Maybe Richard Prentice is footing the bill," Sophie said. "In exchange for a few 'favors.'"

"I don't know."

They headed to a building marked Welcome Center. "We're here to see Phillip Starling," Lauren said.

The receptionist consulted her computer. "He's in Pod A." She indicated a map on the desk in front of her. "Follow this walkway around back and you'll see the groups of cottages are labeled. He's probably in the courtyard. We encourage our guests to spend as much time as possible out of doors, enjoying nature."

Lauren thanked her and they headed down the walk she'd indicated. "What's the difference between a patient and a guest?" Lauren asked.

"Maybe a couple thousand dollars a day?" Sophie guessed.

They found Pod A and walked under a stone archway into a courtyard with padded loungers and shaded tables arranged around a gurgling fountain. Phil, his back to them, sat at one of the tables, talking with a young woman who stood beside a cart next to the table.

As Lauren and Sophie drew nearer, the woman laughed and playfully swatted Phil's shoulder. "You are so bad," she chided.

"Come back after you get off and I'll show you how bad—and how good—I can be," he said.

She laughed again, then saw the two women. "I'd better go," she said, and rolled her cart away.

"Hello, Phil," Lauren said.

He turned toward her and arched one eyebrow. "You're about the last person I expected to see here."

Hair cut, clean shaven and wearing a polo shirt and pressed khakis, he looked much better than the last time she'd seen him. He had a tan and had put on a few pounds. Her ex-husband was definitely handsome. She waited for the catch in her throat that always happened when she saw him again after time apart, and was relieved when it didn't come. Maybe she was finally getting over him. "You're looking good," she said.

"You, too." He stood and kissed her cheek, and nodded to her sister. "Hello, Sophie."

"Hello, Phil." Her greeting was cool; Sophie had never liked Phil, and when he'd left Lauren for another woman she'd stopped trying to hide her disdain.

"What brings you two here?" he asked. "Did you miss me?"

"We wanted to talk to you about Richard Prentice," Lauren said. No sense being coy.

Some of the cheerfulness went out of his eyes, replaced by edgy caution. "What about him?"

"The grand jury refused to indict him on charges of kidnapping," Sophie said.

Phil's surprise seemed genuine. "They think he didn't do it?"

"Apparently, he persuaded them I made up the whole story," Lauren said.

"That's too bad," he said. "I'm sorry to hear it."

"Oh, please." Sophie folded her arms across her chest and glared at him. "Your comments in the paper—calling Prentice your good friend and practically accusing Lauren of being delusional—didn't help matters any."

"You know how the press can be," he said. "Always taking things out of context."

"Did Prentice pay you to say those things about me?" Lauren asked.

"Is that what you think?" He put his hand on her shoulder. She resisted the urge to shrug him off. "Lauren, honey, I know this is hard for you to hear, but you have to admit that the last few months we were together, you were pretty out there. Not yourself."

"Neither of us was at our best then," she said.

"Maybe so. But at least I didn't suddenly decide to redecorate the whole condo and stay up for two nights in a row ripping out tile and moving furniture, only to abandon the project half-done two days later and start looking at new places instead. And what about the time you bought all that expensive cookware and enrolled in an Italian cooking course? You gave one dinner party, then almost never went into the kitchen again."

Lauren did move away from him then. "None of those things hurt anyone," she said.

"They're not normal, Lauren. All I wanted was a normal marriage. A normal life."

"So that's why you became a drug addict," Sophie said. "So things would be 'normal.'"

He took a step toward her, but Lauren stepped between them. "Back to Richard Prentice. Why did you tell the paper he was such a good friend? You hardly knew him."

"I figured it wouldn't hurt my reputation to be associated with a billionaire, you know?"

"How does Prentice feel, being associated with you?" Sophie asked.

Phil shot her a look and turned back to Lauren. "Maybe you shouldn't be going around asking questions about Richard Prentice," he said. "I mean, haven't you had enough trouble from him?"

"Have you talked to him?" she asked. "Did he say anything about me?"

"I didn't have to talk to him," he said. "All I had to do was look him in the eye. There are dark things going on in that brain of his." He took her arm. "Let's take a walk." He glanced at Sophie. "Just the two of us."

She hesitated.

"Please. We need to talk."

"Go on." Sophie sat at the table. "I'll wait here."

He led Lauren down a path, out of the courtyard into an open area at the back of the compound. Beyond the center's manicured grounds stretched open prairie, the mountains blue shadows in the distance. "It's very peaceful here," Lauren said.

"Yeah." He let go of her and hugged his arms across his chest, squinting in the bright sun. "All this openness makes me nervous, though. A lot of times I feel as if people are watching me." He laughed, a hollow sound. "I think paranoia is one of the side effects of withdrawal, or maybe of some of the medication I'm on." He laughed again. "I guess you and me have more in common than I thought."

"What do you mean?"

"We're both messed up in the head."

"Phil, I—"

He shook his head. "Let's not argue. I brought you back here because I just wanted to say I'm sorry things didn't work out between us. I believe we really did love each other and I hope we can be friends going forward."

"What about your girlfriend?" she asked.

He grimaced. "She didn't stick around." He shoved both hands into his pockets and stared out toward the mountains. "Things are going to be better now. This is a good program and I'm getting it together. My agent has some feelers out. I'm thinking of getting into the movies, or maybe television. I could do really well there."

"I'm glad to hear it," she said. "How did you find this place?"

"A friend pulled some strings and got me in."

"Richard Prentice."

He turned to her. "I'm beginning to think the papers are right and you are obsessed with the guy. Let it go, Lauren."

"I won't let it go. Did Richard pay you off to say bad things about me?"

He glanced from side to side, then leaned toward her, his voice low. "He might have shot a little money my way. But I didn't say anything to that reporter that wasn't true. I just maybe exaggerated."

"What do you know about him and Alan Milbanks?" she asked.

He blinked, and for a moment his face went slack. But he recovered, his expression wary. "What about Milbanks?"

"You bought drugs from him."

"What are you now, a cop?" He stepped back. "Yeah, I made a few buys from him."

"Did you ever see him with Richard Prentice?"

"No. He mentioned Prentice to me once. I don't remember how the subject came up—mutual friends or something like that."

Goose bumps prickled her skin in spite of the sun's heat. "Did you tell the police this?"

"No." He shook his head. "Why would I? Anyway, it was no big deal."

"It could be a very big deal. It's another way to link Milbanks and Prentice. It's the kind of evidence that could help bring him to trial for his crimes."

"I told you. You need to let it go." He took another step back. "Get out of it while you can. Move on with your life."

"I can't move on. Not while he goes unpunished for all the wrong he's done. Please. Come back inside with me and we'll make some calls."

He shook his head and put more distance between them. "No way. I've said too much already I—"

Whatever he was going to say was cut off by the whine of a bullet and a dull thud as it slammed into his body. He dropped to his knees and looked up at her, mouth open and eyes wide in surprise as blood bloomed on his chest. Lauren screamed, then turned and ran, her heart pounding in terror.

Chapter Six

The sign over the entrance to Dayspring Wellness Center welcomed visitors to "a dayspring of new beginnings." But Phil Starling had met his end there.

"A single shot from a high-powered rifle. Looks as if it got him right through the heart." The Grand Junction police detective squinted across the empty prairie behind the lot where crime scene personnel swarmed around Starling's slumped body. "There's a shooting range over there. We sent some officers to interview people."

"This wasn't random," Marco said. Sophie had called him as soon as she'd heard what happened. Rand and Lotte had been summoned to assist with the search for a child who'd wandered away from her family's campsite in the park, but Marco had come as soon as he could.

The detective's expression didn't change.

"Do you know someone who wanted this guy dead?"

Richard Prentice. Sophie had told him the sisters had come to the drug treatment center to question Phil about his relationship with the billionaire. But that wasn't enough basis to accuse a man of murder. "Who was footing the bill for Starling's stay here?" Marco asked. "Maybe they were tired of paying."

The detective nodded. "We'll find out. And he was an addict—maybe someone he knew from when he was doing drugs had it in for him. But you see a lot of random things in this job. We'll check the shooting range. We'll also follow any leads we get about suspicious persons."

"Let me know what you find," Marco said. He left the detective and made his way to the secluded courtyard where Sophie and Lauren waited. They sat together on an iron bench, Lauren folded in on herself, huddled with her arms around her waist, her hair falling forward to obscure her face.

Sophie looked up at his approach. "What did you find out?" she asked.

"Let's talk over here," he said, indicating the shade of a tree a few feet away. Lauren didn't even look up when her sister left her. She had yet to acknowledge Marco's presence.

"How is she?" he asked, when Sophie joined him under the tree.

"I've asked one of the doctors here for a sedative. Stress isn't good for her, and something like this…" She shook her head. "It's so awful."

"Did she say what they were talking about, before he was shot?"

"No. He asked to speak to her alone and left me here. So it wasn't an accident?"

The question had a pleading quality. People wanted things like this to be accidents. As tragic as random violence was, it was easier to deal with than the idea of deliberate evil. "There's a shooting range behind here, but I don't think this was an accident." The shot had been too accurate, a shot that killed quickly.

"I never even liked him much, but I never wanted him dead. And to die like that, right in front of Lauren…"

He glanced at the bench again. Lauren was sitting up now, staring into the distance, eyes glazed, her beautiful face a mask of grief. "Did she still love him?" He hadn't meant to ask the question; her feelings were none of his business. But he held his breath, waiting for the answer.

"I loved what we used to have together," Lauren said, her voice husky and low. "I loved the idea of us together, of being married and happy. Of being normal."

He moved to sit beside her on the bench, wanting to touch her, but not touching. "I know this is painful," he said softly. "But I need to know what Phil said to you. What were you talking about before he died?"

"He told me Alan Milbanks talked to him about Richard." Her voice grew stronger and she turned toward him, her knees brushing his leg. "The two of them definitely knew each other. I was trying to persuade him to go to the police, to tell them everything he knew. Someone killed him to keep him quiet, I'm sure of it."

"Was anyone nearby who could have overheard your conversation?" he asked.

"No. But Phil said he felt like someone was watching him. He joked that paranoia was a side effect of his treatment, but maybe he was right and someone was watching. Maybe they could read lips or maybe…maybe just seeing the two of us together was enough for them to kill him." Her voice broke and she bent her head.

Marco gripped her hand. "This may have had nothing to do with you," he said. "Someone decided to silence Phil, for whatever reason. It could have been a drug dealer he owed money or something completely unrelated to our case. Don't waste time blaming yourself."

She sniffed and nodded. "You're right. My falling apart doesn't help anyone."

He squeezed her hand and released it, then stood as a young woman in purple scrubs approached. "Dr. Winstead prescribed this sedative for Ms. Starling." She held out a small paper cup containing a pill, and a paper cup of water.

"Thank you, but I don't need it now." Lauren stood and pushed her hair back from her face. "I just want to go home."

"The local police may want to question you," Marco said.

"Detective Cargill spoke with Dr. Winstead and said he would question Ms. Starling later, when she's feeling better," the nurse said.

"Then, I'll take you home," Marco said.

"I can take her." Sophie put her arm around Lauren.

"I'll follow you and make sure you settle in all right," Marco said.

"Thank you," Lauren said. "I'd appreciate that."

He would have preferred to have Lauren in the car with him for the drive back to Montrose, but he realized she'd probably be more comfortable with her sister. He had to be content with following their car, observing what he could through the windshield. The two women didn't seem to be talking much. Was that a good or a bad sign? His impression was that women always talked more, especially when something was bothering them.

His phone rang. He answered it and Graham's voice boomed over the line. "What's going on over there?"

"Starling died almost instantly, from a single bullet to the heart. He and Lauren were talking in the back garden of the treatment center when he was shot."

"Who shot him? Any suspects?"

"Looks like a sniper. The police are questioning people at a shooting range not far away, but this doesn't look like an accident to me. I think someone wanted to shut him up."

"One of his drug connections?"

"Maybe. Or maybe Prentice. Lauren said they were talking about Prentice when Phil was shot. He told her Prentice and Alan Milbanks knew each other. She was trying to persuade him to tell the police what he knew."

"How is she doing?"

He studied the back of her head in the car ahead of him. She looked so still—too still. "She's had a shock," he said. "A doctor at the center persuaded the local cops to put off their interview until later. I don't think she's going to be able to tell them much anyway. She says she didn't see anything."

"Where are you now?"

"Headed to her apartment. She and Sophie are in Sophie's car, just ahead of me."

"Stay as long as you need to. Make sure the place is secure."

"Yes, sir."

He knew he'd be staying awhile when he followed Sophie's car into the parking lot of their apartment building and found it crowded with vehicles, including two news vans with satellite dishes on their roofs. Reporters lined the walkway leading to the sisters' apartment.

His phone rang, and when he answered it he wasn't surprised to hear Sophie's voice, agitated. "Marco, what are we going to do? How are we going to get past those vultures?"

"Is there a back way in?"

"There's a sliding door onto a patio, but the gate and the door are locked."

"Then, we'll have to go in the front. Stick close to me and don't respond to anything, no matter what the reporters ask."

They parked as close to the apartment as they could get, behind the news vans. Marco exited his Cruiser, then opened Lauren's door and helped her out while Sophie came around from the driver's side. With an arm around each woman, he made his way toward the apartment.

When the reporters spotted them, they swarmed around. Lauren angled her body toward his and buried her face in his shoulder. "Ms. Starling, what do you have to say about your husband's shooting?"

"Are they thinking this is a murder?"

"What were you doing at the treatment center? Were you and Phil planning a reconciliation?"

Marco forced his way through the crowd of clamoring men and women, his fierce expression causing more than one of them to stumble back out of the way. He waited while Sophie unlocked the door, then the three of them hurried inside, the reporters' shouts muffled by the slamming door.

"That was awful," Sophie said as she hurried to draw the drapes across the front window.

"They're just doing their jobs," Lauren said. "Trying to get the story." She moved out of Marco's arms. He was surprised at how empty he felt when she moved away, cold in the absence of her warmth.

"I'll make some tea," Sophie said, and retreated to the kitchen.

Lauren sat on the couch and kicked off her

shoes, revealing pink-polished toenails. "Thank you," she said. "We would have had a tougher time getting through that gauntlet without you."

He sat in a chair across from her. "How are you feeling?" he asked.

She looked pale, but calmer than before. "I'm not sure," she said. "I think I'm still in shock."

"It was a terrible thing to have to experience."

She hugged a pillow to her chest. "Have you ever seen someone shot before?"

"Yes."

"Abby said you were in Special Forces. I guess you've seen a lot of horrible things."

"Yes." Much of his life he'd spent surrounded by violence—in the midst of gang warfare as a child growing up in Los Angeles, as a soldier in Iraq and Afghanistan and as an officer with the DEA.

"How do you handle it without falling apart?" she asked.

"You learn to wall off your emotions. To not see everything that's there."

"That sounds like an awful way to live."

"Maybe it is."

"All my life I've been accused of being too emotional," she said. "Too sensitive. But I'd rather be that way than not feel anything."

She looked him in the eye, a piercing gaze that made him feel naked in front of her. Exposed. "I feel things," he said. He was feeling a lot of things now—a potent mix of lust and admiration and sympathy and the desire to protect her from anything that threatened her. "But I've learned not to show my feelings."

"I'm the opposite." She set the pillow aside. "I can never hide my feelings. I don't know if that's part of my disease, or just the way I'm wired."

"That's one of the things I like about you," he said. "You're honest. I never have to guess your motives."

"You think that now, but you haven't seen me at my worst."

"I've seen a lot of bad things in my life, but you're not one of them."

She shook her head. "Don't go there, Marco."

"Go where?"

"Don't get involved with me. I'm too much trouble. Too unpredictable."

"Maybe I like unpredictable."

"You might think that, but you wouldn't. Phil reminded me of some of the things I did while we were married. I see now how hard I made it for him."

"That wasn't you. It was your disease."

"They're one and the same. I can't separate the two. For better or worse—like a bad marriage. Except there's no chance of divorce."

He leaned toward her, elbows on his knees,

hands clasped in front of him. "You won't convince me you're a bad person," he said. "You're a strong woman, but I'm even stronger. And I like a challenge."

"Why do you care so much?" Her voice rose, angry.

Better anger than despair, he thought. "We have more in common than you think."

Her eyes widened. "Don't tell me you're bipolar, too."

"No. But what you're going through right now—fighting for your reputation against someone who's trying to take you down… I've been there."

She looked skeptical.

He hadn't meant to tell her this; he never talked to anyone about what had happened. He searched for the right words to tell his story as briefly and unemotionally as possible. "When I was first in Iraq, I transferred into a new squadron, so I was the new guy," he said. "For whatever reason, another guy, more senior, decided he didn't like me. He started spreading rumors about me—that I'd been transferred out of my old unit because I was a coward who put other soldiers in danger because I didn't back them up on a mission. It's probably the worst thing you can say about a soldier. Being part of a team means always looking out for the other team members."

"You're not a coward," she said.

"None of these people knew me, so they didn't recognize what the other guy was saying as lies."

"What did you do?"

"I had to prove myself—over and over again. Eventually, the others saw what I was really like, but it took a long time."

"That must have been awful," she said.

"It was, but I got through it. And you'll get through this, too."

"We'll all get through this," Sophie said. She carried a tray into the room and set it on the coffee table between them. She handed Lauren a cup of tea. "There's tea for you, too, Marco, if you want it. But if you need to leave, I understand. Lauren and I will be all right."

"I'm going to stay here tonight, just to be sure," he said.

"That really isn't necessary," she said.

"It's all right," Lauren said. "I'll feel better with you here. In the morning, we can talk about what we're going to do next."

MARCO SPENT THE night on the sofa while Lauren took a sleeping pill that knocked her out for six hours. After she forced herself out of bed and into the shower, she joined Sophie and Marco in the kitchen. They had the newspaper spread out in front of them. Sophie jumped up when Lauren came into the room. "Good morning," she said. "Let me get you some coffee." As she spoke, she folded the section of the paper she'd been reading, then tried to take Marco's from him.

"Leave the paper," Lauren said. She sat in the chair to Marco's left. "I want to see what they have to say."

Sophie bit her bottom lip, her hand still protectively atop the stack of papers.

"Let her see," Marco said. "She needs to know what we're up against."

"I'll get the coffee," Sophie said, and hurried away.

"How are you feeling this morning?" Marco asked, his dark eyes fixed on her. He needed a shave and had slept in his clothes, but the ruggedness only made him look sexier.

"I've felt better," she said. "But I'll be okay." She'd taken her medication and done some of the centering exercises her therapist had given her. At the first sign of anything off-kilter, she would call her doctor. She was determined to stay in control and on top of this.

He slid a section of paper toward her. "Start here," he said. "Some of it's pretty ugly, though."

She took a deep breath. "I'm getting used to that."

The front page of the *Post* featured a shot from her wedding, Lauren in a white veil and gown, carrying a bouquet of roses, Phil in a black tux with a white rose boutonniere. He'd been smiling at the camera while she smiled at him. Maybe a foreshadowing of how their marriage would turn out. The headline over the shot proclaimed Actor Murdered in Front of Ex.

Sophie handed Lauren a cup of coffee and returned to her chair. "The reporter who wrote that article should get a job with the tabloids," she said. "He manages to include every bit of gossip and innuendo he could find."

Lauren scanned the article, which began with the facts—Phil had been shot while standing in the back garden of the treatment center with his ex-wife, who had come to visit him. He was undergoing treatment for drug addiction. Prior to that, he had worked as an actor with a Denver theater company and won several awards for his work. His ex was a popular former Channel 9 news anchor who had a history of mental illness. She had been in the news lately for accusing prominent billionaire Richard Prentice of trying to kill her. The morning of the shooting, a grand jury had failed to indict Prentice for the crimes.

Okay, nothing here she hadn't expected, though she would have preferred the reporter be more specific with her diagnosis. She had bipolar disorder, a fairly common, controllable disease. She wasn't a psychopath, a sociopath, or suffering from any of the other sometimes dangerous disorders that people associated with criminal behavior. She continued reading, but the next sentence made her freeze. "Given her history of erratic behavior, police have not ruled out Ms. Starling as a suspect in her ex-husband's death."

She read the words out loud, her voice breaking on the last syllable. Sophie leaned across the table and covered her hand. "I didn't want you to see that," she said.

"How could anyone think I had anything to do with Phil's murder?" she asked. "I was standing right there when he was shot—by a sniper who wasn't anywhere near."

"I spoke with Detective Cargill this morning," Marco said. "Someone at the scene speculated that the crime could have been a murder for hire and apparently the reporter took that and ran with it."

"What kind of sicko would hire an assassin,

then arrange to be with the intended victim when he died?" Sophie asked.

"Apparently the kind of sicko some people think I am." Lauren pushed the paper away and reached for the coffee with shaking hands. "What else did the police say?"

"They're still questioning people at the gun range," Marco said. "The trajectory of the bullet indicates it was fired from there, or near there."

"They don't really think this was an accident, do they?" Sophie asked.

He shrugged, an elegant movement of his shoulders that made Lauren think of an exotic wild animal—a cheetah or a panther. Like one of those big cats, he seemed so calm and contained, sitting there beside her. Yet underneath the stillness lay something lethal, poised to unleash itself if the situation called for it.

"If they think this is an accident, the police might not take the crime as seriously," Lauren said. "Even if they find the shooter, they won't look into who might have hired him to do the shooting."

"This feels like a professional hit to me," Marco said. "They won't find him."

"So we'll never know if Richard Prentice was behind this or not." The truth of that statement shouldn't have surprised her. Though the

Rangers could link people engaged in everything from prostitution to drug trafficking to Prentice, the billionaire always managed to distance himself. Some pointed to this as proof of his innocence, but having spent six weeks as his prisoner, Lauren could never believe it. He had never mistreated her; he'd pampered her, even. But his determination to make her his own, in spite of her protests, had shown her the twisted soul beneath the tailored suits and calm demeanor.

"What are we going to do now?" she asked.

"I don't want you leaving the house alone." Marco shifted his gaze to include Sophie. "Either of you."

"Why?" Sophie asked. "You don't really think we're in danger, do you? The grand jury let Prentice go."

"That sniper killed Phil," Marco said. "But the shooter could just as easily have targeted Lauren."

"Richard said he loved me. He wanted me to marry him. In his twisted way, I think he meant what he said. He wants to frighten me into keeping quiet, but I can't believe he wants me dead. I don't think he wants me dead." But the memory of Phil falling at her feet, blood blooming at his chest, sent an icy chill through her, and she had to set aside the coffee. "What am I supposed to do?" she asked. "I can't hide in here forever."

"The offer still stands for you to come stay with me," he said. "And Sophie could move in with Rand."

"I appreciate the offer, but that's no real solution," she said. "I wouldn't be able to come and go at your place, either, and I'd feel guilty about inconveniencing you."

"That's really sweet of you, Marco," Sophie said. "But Lauren doesn't need the stress of trying to get comfortable in a new place. She needs routine and familiarity and calm."

Right. And the last thing she wanted was for Marco to see her when she wasn't coping well.

"Then, you can stay here," he relented. "But don't go out unless I can be with you. Or Rand or one of the other Rangers."

"You couldn't protect me from a sniper," she said.

"Maybe not, but I can keep you safe from other closer attacks."

She believed he wanted to protect her, and the idea touched her more than she wanted to admit. But how could one man, even a law enforcement officer who'd been in Special Forces, protect her from an enemy she couldn't see and wasn't even sure she knew? "I heard the captain yesterday—you have work to do," she said. "You probably shouldn't even be here now."

"After the shooting yesterday, I'm sure the captain would agree protecting you is important to our case."

The captain might also think she was more trouble than she was worth.

A knock on the door made them all jump. Marco quickly moved to the window and pulled back the curtain a scant inch. Then he relaxed. "It's Rand."

He opened the door and Sophie embraced her lover, who was dressed casually this morning in khakis and a blue polo shirt. "Where's Lotte?" Lauren asked. She didn't often see Rand without the police dog.

"She's at the groomer's. Technically, it's our day off, though I'm still working on the case."

"Marco's been scaring us with all his warnings about danger," Sophie said.

"I hope it worked." He kissed her cheek, then nodded to Lauren. "What's the latest?" he asked Marco.

"The Grand Junction police think the bullet came from that firing range behind the treatment center," Marco said.

Rand nodded. "Perfect place for the shooter to blend in. By the time anyone figured out he was aiming at more than the range targets, he could be long gone."

"Any new developments on your end?" Marco asked.

"Prentice gave another press conference this morning in Denver, where he's attending a board meeting or something. Senator Mattheson was with him and they took turns going on about what a nuisance The Ranger Brigade is to public safety and how much we are costing the taxpayers every day we're allowed to continue our efforts to usurp local authority."

"He said *usurp*?" Marco asked.

"That and a lot of other five-dollar words. The reporters were eating it up, from what I could see of the television footage."

"How did the captain react?" Marco asked.

"He looked as though he wanted to cut out Prentice's liver and eat it for lunch. But he'd never let anyone outside the Rangers see how upset he is."

"The press will have us under the microscope now," Marco said. "Waiting for us to make one wrong move."

"Speaking of being under the microscope, did you know someone is watching this place?" Rand asked.

"It's probably one of those reporters," Sophie said. "When we got back from Grand Junction last night there must have been a dozen of them camped out by the door."

"The reporters were gone when I checked this morning," Marco said.

"Come check this out." They all followed Rand to the kitchen window. "The gray SUV, parked on the corner," he said.

Marco stood a few inches back from the window and looked in the direction Rand indicated. Lauren came to stand behind him, her hand on his broad, warm back. Touching him this way made her feel steadier—anchored. "It looks like a regular car to me," she said.

"Look again," Rand said. "There's a guy in it and he's definitely keeping an eye on this place."

"Not the same one who was watching you the other day," Marco said. He moved toward the door, Rand close behind him. "Let's find out what this guy is up to."

Chapter Seven

Shoulder to shoulder, Lauren and Sophie stood at the window and watched Rand and Marco saunter down the street—two friends on their way to get coffee or take in a movie, deep in conversation as they walked. When the Rangers reached the SUV, they suddenly veered over, one on each side of the vehicle. Marco leaned in and said something, and then the driver got out of the vehicle.

"Anybody you know?" Sophie asked.

Lauren shook her head. "He's not one of Richard's guards." They were all big, strong men. This guy was slight and at least six inches shorter than Marco. He had thinning brown hair in need of a trim and dark-framed nerd glasses.

The man was gesticulating now, hands waving, head shaking. Marco and Rand said little, listening. "I wish we could hear what they're saying," Sophie said.

"Nobody looks upset," Lauren said. Rand and Marco were alert, but not rigidly tense. Rand was even smiling now.

After a moment, the man handed Marco something, got in his car and drove away.

The two Rangers made their way back to the apartment. The women met them at the door. "Who is he?" Lauren asked.

"What did he want?" Sophie chimed in.

Marco closed the door behind him, then handed Lauren a card.

"Andrew Combs. Co-Lar Productions," she read, then gave Marco a questioning look. "I don't get it."

"He says he runs an online news network. He wants to offer you a job as their news anchor."

"The face of *Exposed News*," Rand said.

"Exposed News?" She made a face. "I've never heard of it."

"There's a website listed on the card," Marco said. "He certainly made it sound legit."

"If he's so legit, why is he parked out there spying on us?" Sophie asked.

"He said he knew reporters had been hassling you and he didn't want you to think he was one of them," Rand said. "So he planned to wait until you came out to run errands or something, and he'd meet up with you then."

"On neutral ground," Marco said.

"And he said he wanted to offer me a job. For real?"

"He said he could offer you top pay and all kinds of media exposure," Rand said. "That he'd take your career in a new direction."

"That sounds great," Sophie said. "And online, it would be a national audience, right? Not just Denver. This could be a great thing for you."

Sophie's enthusiasm was contagious. Lauren stared at the card, a giddy feeling of excitement bubbling up in her chest. She did have a lot of experience. Maybe this could be a big break. "Let's take a look at the website," she said.

They trooped to her laptop on the coffee table. She booted up the computer, then brought up the browser and typed in the address for *Exposed News*. "You must be eighteen or older to view this website," came the warning page. "That's strange," she said.

"Maybe they're just being overly cautious," Sophie said. "I mean, news is full of sex and violence, right? Probably not something you want little kids accidentally surfing to."

Lauren clicked the box to verify she was over eighteen and hit Enter. A video loaded, and after a moment they were staring at an attractive young woman reading a report on fighting in the Middle East.

"Am I hallucinating, or is she naked?" Sophie asked.

"Definitely naked," Rand said.

"Yep," Marco said. "Fully exposed."

LAUREN BEGAN TO LAUGH. Not the hysterical laughter of someone on the verge of losing it, but a melodic chuckle that flooded Marco with warmth. He smiled, and the others joined in the laughter.

"It's nice to know I have something I can fall back on," Lauren said. She shut down the website. "But I don't think I'm ready for naked news just yet."

"No wonder the guy was nervous about talking to you," Sophie said. "The idea is so ridiculous."

"Life is pretty ridiculous sometimes," Lauren said. "Or haven't you noticed?" She turned to Marco. "What now? I know you said you didn't want us going out alone, but the two of you must have work to do."

"I don't think you should stay here alone, either," he said. "This apartment is too vulnerable."

"What do you mean?" Sophie asked.

"It's too accessible from the front and the

back," Rand said. "The front door isn't reinforced. Almost anyone could kick it in. You don't have an alarm system or a security camera focused on the door."

"We should go back to our original plan of you two staying with us until we're sure the danger has passed," Marco said.

"It will be easier for us to work if we know you're somewhere safe," Rand said.

Marco looked away from the tender expression his friend directed at Sophie. He might have said the same words to Lauren, except he wasn't one for expressing his feelings in public. Not that he knew exactly what his feelings for the beautiful newscaster were. He'd been assigned to protect her the day he rescued her from Prentice's ranch and he still felt obligated to that duty, but there was something else going on between the two of them that he hadn't yet figured out. Physical attraction definitely played a part, but he also felt an emotional connection with her he hadn't experienced with any other woman. His natural inclination was to back off and not pursue his feelings any further, but the more time he spent with Lauren, the more difficult to do he found that.

"Pack what you need for a few days and come with us," Rand continued. "If you hate it, we'll try to find a safe house or some other place you can stay."

"All right." Sophie took Lauren's hand. "Come on. It can't hurt to go along with them." She winked at Rand. "It might even be fun."

While the women prepared to leave, Marco and Rand went outside to wait. Rand leaned against the side of the building, hands in his pockets, and gazed across the half-empty parking lot. "Naked news." He chuckled. "It would definitely make dull stories about politics and economics more exciting."

Marco tensed, waiting for his friend to say something about Lauren being a good fit for the job, but Rand was smart enough not to go there. Instead, Marco's own mind conjured an image of a naked Lauren reading a news story. His mind went fuzzy as he focused on this picture of her gorgeous breasts and shapely hips…

With great effort, he forced his mind away from the enticing fantasy and discreetly shifted position to accommodate the erection the daydream had produced. "It's a crazy idea," he muttered, and turned away.

After a moment the women emerged, suitcases in hand. "I'll take Sophie to Ranger headquarters with me," Rand said. "Carmen and I are going back over all the evidence we collected at Prentice's ranch the night we rescued

Lauren. We're hoping we can find something to counter the stories Prentice has been floating in the press, and tie him to criminal activity."

"I want to stop by the motel where Phil was staying before he went into rehab," Marco said.

"We'll meet you at the station when I'm done there."

"What are you hoping to learn at the motel?" Lauren asked when she was buckled into the passenger seat of Marco's Cruiser.

"I'm curious who might have visited Phil while he was in town."

The motel was a low-slung, old-fashioned motor court, the white paint faded and flaking. The doors to the rooms, each set back slightly from the next in line, had once been blue, though that, too, had faded to almost gray. Marco parked the Cruiser in front of the office.

"I hadn't imagined it would be this bad," Lauren said.

"Not his usual style?"

She shook her head. "I guess he really was in financial trouble." Her eyes grew shiny and she blinked back tears. "I'm sorry." She ducked her head. "It's just hard, realizing he's gone."

Marco handed her a handkerchief. "He was a big part of your life," he said. The words sounded inadequate, but he couldn't bring himself to say more. He knew Lauren and Phil had been married for seven years, but he hated to admit she'd loved a guy like that—one who was so weak.

She dabbed at her eyes, careful not to smear her makeup. "Things were over between us a long time ago," she said. "But I still cared about him. Not the way I cared when we were first married, but just because he'd been important to me once." She glanced at him. "Have you ever been married?"

"No."

"Why not?"

He could have told her the answer was none of her business, or dismissed the question with a cliché about not having met the right woman. But too many people had lied to Lauren; he didn't want to be one of them. "The work I do is dangerous. Adding someone else into the mix, someone I care about and need to protect, complicates things. I might make a mistake because I'm thinking of that person instead of the job."

"Or maybe knowing that person was supporting you, wanting you to come home safely, would inspire you to even greater success." She folded the handkerchief and handed it back to him. "I don't think relationships are ever all good or all bad. Sometimes it's a matter of perspective."

No one had ever skewed his perspective the way she had; he didn't know if he liked it or not. He tucked the handkerchief back into his pocket and opened the door of the Cruiser. "Let's go see who we can find to talk to."

The only person in the office was an older man in a stained white T-shirt. He scowled at the badge Marco showed him, glanced at Lauren, then back at Marco. "What do you want?" he asked.

"You had a man staying here for almost four weeks in June and July," Marco said. "Phil Starling."

"Don't know him."

"Maybe this will refresh your memory." Marco handed over a copy of that morning's paper with Phil's photo and the news of his death on the front page.

The old man grunted. "Him. So he got shot." He shoved the paper back across the counter. "Nothing to do with me."

"I want to know if anyone came to see him while he was here," Marco said.

"What? You think I keep tabs on my guests? What they do is their own business."

Marco glanced out the window to the right of the front desk, at the row of rooms with blue doors. "You've got a pretty good view here. You strike me as a man who keeps an eye on things."

The man stood up a little straighter. "I don't want any trouble. I run a clean place."

"So you would have noticed if Mr. Starling had visitors."

"He didn't. He kept to himself."

"So no one ever came to see him the whole time he was here?" Marco asked.

"I didn't say that. People stopped by a couple times."

"What kind of people? Can you describe them?"

The guy shrugged. "A couple of big fellows. Football linebacker types."

"How many times did they visit?"

"What's it to you?"

"We're trying to find out who killed him." Not exactly true. That case belonged to the Grand Junction cops. Marco was looking for any connection to Richard Prentice, who was known to hire beefy guys as his private security guards. "How many times did these big guys come to see Phil Starling?"

The old man looked down at the newspaper. "Twice. Once a few days before Starling moved out. The second time, he left with them, but not before one came in and paid his bill."

"How much was the bill?"

"One hundred and seventy-three dollars with tax. I was ready to throw the bum out for being so behind. He kept telling me he'd get the money, and I guess he was right."

"Did the man who paid say anything?" Marco asked. "Did he give you a name or say who he worked for or anything?" They should be so lucky.

"No. He just asked how much Starling owed and paid up. Cash, from a big wad of bills."

"You didn't think that was unusual, to pay in cash?"

"Some people don't like credit cards."

"Did Starling leave anything behind in his room when he moved out?" Marco asked.

"No. I was expecting it to be trashed, he'd been holed up in there so long, but they must have taken everything with them. Even the garbage. It was clean. I mean, cleaner than it was when he checked in. Looked as if somebody had washed everything in there."

"Anything else you can tell us about Phil Starling?" Marco asked.

"Nope."

Marco handed him a business card. "If you think of anything, call me at that number."

Lauren waited until they were in the Cruiser once more before she spoke. "Phil wasn't that fastidious," she said. "He never cleaned when we were married."

"His two friends might have done the job."

"But why go to all that trouble?"

"I don't know. Maybe to get rid of fingerprints, or anything that betrayed their identity."

"They sound like the type of guys who work for Richard," she said.

"Unless we find something to prove an association, that doesn't do us any good," he said.

"It's so frustrating, how he never does his own dirty work," she said. "His money and his position keep him a safe distance from anything incriminating."

He backed the Cruiser out of the parking spot and turned onto the street. "In this case, there's nothing criminal about paying someone's hotel bill," he said.

"Then, why do it?" she asked. "I can't believe it's because he liked Phil so much."

"Favors like that make people obligated to him," Marco said. "When he needs something from them, they're more likely to go along."

"That's a lot of trouble to go to just to get someone to tell reporters I'm crazy." Her voice cracked and Marco glanced at her, wondering if she was going to cry again. But she stiffened her shoulders and stared straight ahead. "I still can't believe Richard might want to kill me now. He said he loved me."

"His mind is twisted. Unpredictable."

She plucked at the seat belt and worried her lower lip between her teeth. "It was so strange. The whole time I was at his ranch," she said, "he kept telling me he loved me, but I never really believed him. There was something about him... He was too cold and unemotional. He didn't seem capable of love."

"Some people are harder to read than others." He'd been accused of being incapable of love himself. He sometimes wondered if his accusers were right. A lifetime of schooling his emotions left him sometimes unsure of what he really felt.

"Richard wasn't just reserved," she said. "There's something wrong with him. I don't understand why other people can't see it."

"Maybe you're more sensitive to emotions than other people."

"Because I'm so emotional myself?" She made a face.

"No. Because you have a gift for reading people."

Her expression softened and she turned toward him. "Thank you," she said.

He started to tell her she didn't need to thank him for anything, but her next words silenced him. "I'm not thanking you for the compliment," she said. "Though that was nice, too. I'm thanking you for respecting me. For treating me like a sensible adult. That's something this disease has stolen from me. Once people could put a label on me—bipolar—they started treating me differently, as if I wasn't even me anymore, just this sick person."

"I don't see you as a sick person." She had her problems, but everyone did, whether they were out there for the world to see or not.

"I know. And that means a lot to me."

Silence settled between them, charged with the awareness of things left unsaid. Other men— Rand and Michael Dance and even the captain— found ways to navigate the divide between duty and personal feeling, but he didn't know how to manage that. From the time he was a kid in his first gang, obeying the rules had been what had kept him in line. What kept him alive. The rules said you didn't fraternize with witnesses or the people you were charged with protecting. In real life, it happened all the time, but not to him.

His cell phone rang, and he punched the button to answer it. "Cruz."

"Marco, you need to get back to headquarters as soon as possible." Rand's voice sounded strained.

"What is it?" Marco asked. "What's wrong?"

"I don't know. The captain has called a meeting. He wants everyone here ASAP."

"We're on our way."

"What is it?" Lauren asked after he'd hung up.

"The captain's called a meeting. Maybe he's got some news about the case."

"I hope so. It would be a relief to have at least some answers."

The lot was crowded with Rangers' vehicles. Marco found a parking place at the far end, and he and Lauren joined the others inside. "What's up?" Marco asked Rand.

"I don't know. The captain has been in his office all morning."

They stared at the door to the captain's private office. Just then, it opened, and Graham emerged. He looked solemn, angry even. Whatever he had to say, it wasn't going to be good.

He walked to the front of the room and faced them. A hush fell over the crowd. "There's no easy way to say this, so I'll just get this over with." Graham glanced at a piece of paper in his hand—a printout of some kind. "The justice department issued an order this morning disbanding the interagency task force." He looked up, his face grim. "Effective immediately, The Ranger Brigade is no more."

Chapter Eight

Stunned silence followed Graham's announcement, then everyone started talking at once. Lauren touched Marco's arm. "What does this mean?" she asked. "Were you all just fired?" She certainly knew what that felt like.

"Not exactly," he said. "With the task force dissolved, we go back to our regular positions in law enforcement."

"So you're with the DEA, right?"

He nodded, his expression grim.

She looked around the room, at the other men and women, who seemed equally upset. "What happens to the cases you were investigating?"

"Some of them will be turned over to local law enforcement," he said.

"You mean the Montrose police?"

"Or the sheriff's department, or the Grand Junction police."

"So they'll continue investigating Richard Prentice."

"What do you think?"

"I think the chances of that happening aren't very high." Now that the grand jury had failed to bring charges, local authorities had no reason to pursue the case further. Not unless a new crime was committed or new evidence came to light. Without an ongoing investigation, the chances of finding new evidence seemed slim to none.

Not to mention that the local cops didn't have the manpower or the funds to fight Prentice and his phalanx of lawyers. Most of the people she'd met in her brief time in town before Prentice had kidnapped her were intimidated by the billionaire. He had influence over judges and politicians at a state level. Look at how easily he'd persuaded the courts to drop all the charges the Rangers had brought against him.

"But you can still work on the case, can't you?" she asked, struggling to salvage something positive from this latest news. "I mean, at least the drug part of it. Alan Milbanks was smuggling drugs, and I'm sure Prentice was bankrolling him. I know there's proof out there that Prentice was involved in Milbanks's operation. You can keep looking for that proof."

"You don't understand. I won't be here to investigate anything. My duty post is in Denver."

His words hit her like a physical blow. He was leaving her? Alone?

Rand, Sophie and Michael joined them. They looked as poleaxed by the news as she felt. "This changes everything," Michael said.

But Lauren had had too many changes in her life the past few months. She turned to Rand. "You can stay, can't you?" she asked. "You're with the Bureau of Land Management. They have a lot of land in this part of Colorado."

"I can't guarantee where my bosses will send me." He put his arm around Sophie and drew her close. She looked on the verge of tears. "But if I have to, I'll ask for leave."

"An investigation like this takes more than one person," Michael said. "It takes a team."

"A team like we were," Rand said.

Graham joined them. "Where will you go, Captain?" Lauren asked.

"I've been ordered back to Washington."

"Will Emma go with you?" Michael asked.

His expression grew more strained. "I hope so, but her work is here."

"She'll go with you," Lauren said. "This could be her chance to land a job with one of the big national papers."

"Richard Prentice is going to get away with

murder now that he doesn't have the Rangers watching him," Sophie said. "It makes me so angry."

"I'll still be watching him," Lauren said. "I'm not going to stop digging into his background and looking into his business dealings."

"You can't do that," Sophie said. "It's too dangerous for you to do that stuff on your own."

"She won't be on her own," Marco said.

They all stared at him. "I'll be with you," he said.

"But you just said you had to report to Denver," Lauren said.

"I promised I'd protect you. With the Rangers disbanded, you'll be more vulnerable than ever."

She could hardly believe what he was saying. She swallowed past the knot that had formed in her throat. "But what about your job?"

"As of right now, I'm taking a leave of absence. I have some unfinished business to take care of."

THIS CHANGES EVERYTHING. Michael's words repeated like a mantra in Marco's thoughts as he cleaned out his locker at Ranger headquarters. Around him, the other members of the team were filling duffels and backpacks with personal belongings.

"Simon, is that smell coming from your locker?" Michael called across the room. "What have you got in there?"

"It's my running clothes." Simon held up a handful of T-shirts. "I haven't had time to do laundry lately."

"They ought to be declared hazardous waste," Michael said.

"Maybe I'll leave them here. A little souvenir for whoever has to clean up this place."

Carmen looked up from the locker next to Marco's. "What do you think will happen to this place?" she asked.

"Don't know. They'll probably haul it someplace and use it for storage or offices."

"I called my supervisor in Denver," she said. "Left him a voice mail that I needed to take some personal time."

"You're staying, then?"

She nodded. "I don't like leaving work half-done."

Rand walked by, a duffel in each hand, Lotte by his side. "What about Lotte?" Marco asked.

He stopped; the dog stopped, too. "What about her?"

"Isn't she government property?" Marco asked.

"She's my partner. If I'm on leave, she's on leave."

"You're not worried they'll reassign her?" Carmen asked.

"They'd have to find her first." He turned to Marco. "You realize we have to clear out of the duplex, right?"

"Why would you have to do that?" Carmen asked.

"It's state property," Marco said. "One of the perks of the job."

"I remember now," she said. "I was ticked I didn't get one of those, but now I'm glad they gave me a housing allowance instead. As long as my savings hold out, I can keep my apartment."

"Don't say that too loud," Rand said. "Or you're liable to end up with roommates."

"Uh-uh. It's one bedroom and my cat has already claimed the couch."

Marco stuffed a last notebook into his duffel and zipped it shut. "I'm done here," he said. Time to focus on the future, on finding justice—and justification for the Rangers.

Lauren and Sophie were waiting in the front room. Emma and Abby had joined them, the four gathered in a worried knot by the door, watching the parade of officers and staff carrying boxes and bags to the parking lot. "I can't believe this is happening," Emma said.

"Are you going to write about it for the paper?" Rand asked.

She shook her head. "I couldn't. I'm too outraged for it to ever make it into print."

"Do you think Richard Prentice and Senator Mattheson are celebrating right now?" Lauren asked.

"I hope they are," Rand said. "If they believe we aren't a threat anymore they'll let down their guard."

"How are you going to continue the investigation without access to your files and records?" Abby asked.

"I'll still have access for a few more weeks, at least." Graham joined them. "I'm staying on for a few weeks to oversee the transfer of records, disposal of the building, et cetera," he said. "I'll try to draw it out as long as possible and if you need me to look up anything for you, I will."

"Then, you're okay with what we're doing?" Rand asked.

The lines on Graham's forehead deepened. "I'm not okay with any of this, but I admire your dedication, and I want to finish the job we came here to do—to stop this crime wave that's threatening to take over public lands."

"Why don't you meet at our place this eve-

ning and discuss what you're going to do?"
Emma said.

Graham nodded. "Everyone get settled, then
come to my house at seven."

"Women, too," Emma said. "We can help."

"Women, too," Graham agreed.

"Meanwhile, Marco and I need to collect our
belongings from our duplex before someone
remembers it belongs to the state and locks us
out," Rand said.

"Would they really do that?" Sophie asked.

"I never thought they'd disband the Rangers," he said. "Now I wouldn't put anything
past them."

"Where will you stay?" Emma asked.

"They'll stay with us," Lauren said.

When everyone turned to look at her, she
flushed pink. "I mean, Sophie and Rand are
practically living together already, and we'll
find someplace for Marco…" Her voice trailed
away.

"Of course they'll stay with us." Sophie put
her arm through Rand's.

"You know Lotte has to come with me,"
Rand said. "That's okay, isn't it?" Sophie had
been terrified of the dog when they'd first met.

She nodded. "I'm okay with Lotte, though,
come to think of it, I'm not sure if our complex allows dogs."

"We'll worry about that later." He turned to Marco. "You okay with staying with the girls?"

He nodded, his gaze still focused on Lauren. Maybe she had plans for him to sleep on the sofa. That might work for a night or two, but being in such close proximity to her wasn't going to do anything to lessen the attraction between them. Now that he was on leave, his duty to her was less well defined. Instead of a law officer and a witness, they were just a man and a woman.

As Michael had said, the disbandment of the Rangers changed everything.

Lauren and Sophie headed back to their apartment. They'd persuaded the men they'd be fine for the few hours it took for them to pack and move their stuff into Graham's garage, where he'd offered to store their belongings.

"Rand tried to get me to bring Lotte with us," Sophie said as she drove the car through town. "I'm a lot more comfortable with her than I used to be, but that still doesn't mean I want to be alone with her."

"We can use this time to get ready for the guys," Lauren said.

"And just where is Marco going to sleep? He's too tall for our sofa."

"I'm sure when he was in Special Forces he slept in places that were a lot more uncomfortable than our living room floor. We can make him a pallet or something." Her face felt as if it was on fire, the curse of being fair skinned and blushing easily.

"Okay. If that's what you want." Sophie's smile was more of a smirk. "Though I can think of places he might be more comfortable."

"Stop it, Sophie. We're not even going to go there." Though even as she said the words, heat pooled between her legs at the thought of Marco naked and in her bed. *Stop it*, she ordered herself. She was never going to get through this if she didn't keep her libido under control.

"We'd better stop at the grocery store," she said. "The guys are going to want more to eat than yogurt and frozen diet dinners."

"We also have canned soup and your not-so-secret stash of chocolate," Sophie said.

"Hey, that chocolate is for emergencies!"

"We'd better buy more. I feel more emergencies coming on."

They detoured to the grocery store, where they filled their cart with chips and lunch meat and frozen waffles and anything they considered "guy" food. "They'd better be hungry," Sophie said as she pushed the loaded cart toward their car.

"I just thought of something," Lauren said. "What if they're into health food or something? Maybe they only eat tofu and chicken and salads."

Sophie laughed. "Trust me, Rand will eat his share of junk food—and Marco's share, too, if it comes to that."

"So things seem pretty serious between you two," Lauren said. "Do you think you'll get married?"

"Maybe. We've talked about the future—a little. But neither of us wants to rush into anything."

"Good idea. Maybe if I'd been more cautious, I wouldn't have made such a mistake with Phil."

"You're in a better place now than you were then."

She started to answer, but stopped when she noticed movement beside their car. A tall, broad-shouldered man dressed in black stepped out from the passenger side of a white van parked beside them. Something about him looked so familiar.

A crushing grip around her torso cut off the

thought. She struggled against the man who held her. "Sophie, run!" she screamed, before her assailant's other hand closed over her mouth, silencing her.

Chapter Nine

Lauren clawed at the face of the man who held her, wild with terror. She writhed in his arms and kicked at his shins as hard as she could. He swore and squeezed her tighter, sending pain stabbing through her chest and cutting off her breath until she feared she might black out. On the other side of the car, Sophie struggled with the man Lauren had seen getting out of the van. She rammed the shopping cart into him, then began pulling cans and bottles from the cart and hurling them at him. He ducked and grabbed for her, but she kept the cart between them and screamed at the top of her lungs. "Help! Help! Somebody, help!"

Lauren opened her mouth as wide as she could, then bit down hard on the hand of the man who held her, tasting blood. He yowled and loosened his hold on her, enough that she could free one hand to jab at his eyeball. With another yowl, he released her and she lurched away from him, staggering and gasping for breath.

By this time, Sophie's screams had attracted the attention of other shoppers, who gathered in front of the store. "The police are on their way!" someone shouted.

At this, Sophie's attacker dived back into the van. Lauren's assailant lunged after him, and within seconds they screeched out of the parking lot. Two men and a woman rushed forward to help the sisters, offering water and reassurance, and helping to gather their scattered groceries. Lauren hugged Sophie, tears streaming down both their faces.

A siren announced the arrival of two police cars. The officers, a man and a woman, approached. After determining that Sophie and Lauren were frightened and a little bruised, but not seriously hurt, they asked what had happened.

"We came out of the store with our groceries and two men attacked us," Sophie said.

"They fought like wildcats," one of the bystanders offered. "It was really something."

"Did you know these men?" the male officer asked. "Had you ever seen them before?"

Lauren shook her head. She was pretty sure the man who'd gone after Sophie had worked for Richard Prentice, but she'd share that information with the Rangers, who were more likely to take her seriously.

"The one who went after Sophie was a big guy, with very short blond hair and a cleft chin," she said. "I never saw the guy who went after me, but they were both in a white van. The kind service companies use, but this one didn't have a name or logo or anything on it."

"The man who attacked my sister looked like a wrestler," Sophie said. "Dark hair, not too tall—maybe five-eight or five-nine?"

"Did either of you see a license plate on the van?" the male officer asked.

Lauren shook her head.

"I took a picture," a woman volunteered. She stepped forward to show her cell phone.

The officer studied it. "Looks as if they've smeared mud on the plate, but send it over and our techs will see if they can make out anything."

The officers interviewed bystanders and the store manager, and took down Sophie's and Lauren's contact information. When Lauren gave her name, the female officer did a double take. "You're that newscaster who had that run-in with Richard Prentice," she said.

Lauren stiffened. "Yes."

The officer had very pale, gray eyes and an open, direct gaze. "For what it's worth, I believed you," she said. "But Prentice's money talks pretty loud around here." She tucked her notebook into her pocket. "But you didn't hear that from me."

The male officer joined them. "Will you ladies be all right getting home or would you like one of us to follow you?" he asked.

Lauren hugged her arms across her chest. "It's up to Sophie. I'm definitely too shaky to drive." Now that the adrenaline had faded, she felt almost too weak to stand, and she ached all over.

"Thank you, but we'll be fine," Sophie said, and turned to Lauren. "I texted Rand, and he and Marco are coming to get us."

MARCO KNEW HE had to tamp down the rage that filled him when Rand told him Lauren and Sophie had been attacked in a supermarket parking lot. The women were all right, so the focus now had to be on making sure they were safe. Later, he'd work on finding out who had targeted them and bringing them to justice. *Stay in control and act deliberately, always aware of what the most important task is at the moment. Never let emotion get in the way of doing your job.* These were the lessons that had helped him excel over the years.

But no training or mental discipline could

prepare him for the relief that flooded him when he saw Lauren, shaken but safe, standing in that parking lot. His knees almost buckled when he climbed out of the pickup truck that was Rand's personal vehicle, and he had to stand still for a moment, holding on to the door and trying to recover. The knowledge that she could have been seriously hurt, even killed, shook him to the point he couldn't speak, and he fought the urge to crush her in his arms.

So this was how it's going to be, he told himself, trying to accept this new reality. After years of avoiding caring deeply for anyone, he'd found a woman he quite possibly couldn't live without.

After a few seconds, he recovered enough to join Lauren and the others beside Sophie's car. "Hey," he greeted her. "You okay?"

She nodded, then shook her head. "I've never been so scared in my life."

Pulling her to him was as automatic as breathing. She buried her face against his chest and he smoothed her hair and spoke softly. "It's going to be okay," he said. "You're going to be all right."

"Sophie says the guys who went after them were big, beefy types," Rand said after a moment. "They were in a white van with the tag obscured."

"I recognized one of them." Lauren straightened and brushed her hair back out of her eyes. Her expression was strained, but she looked calm. "The one who attacked Sophie. He worked as a guard for Richard Prentice. His name was Al or Hal or something like that."

"You didn't say anything to the police about that," Sophie said.

"No. I figured the minute I mentioned Richard Prentice they'd discount everything I said. After all, I'm the crazy woman who had such a twisted crush on him that I went to his house and refused to leave. Then, when he didn't return my affections, I accused him of kidnapping me."

"Don't say that." Marco couldn't keep the hardness from his voice. "You're not crazy."

"No, I'm not," she said softly. "But I'm tired of always having to defend myself. I knew if I waited and told you two about the guy, you'd take me seriously."

"A lot of other people saw him," Sophie said. "If we can link him to Prentice, it won't be only your word against his."

"Right now we need to make sure he can't get to you again." One arm still around her, Marco urged her toward Rand's truck.

She halted, stumbling. "Do you think they'll come back?"

"If Prentice sent them to kidnap you again and they failed, they'll try to finish the job," Marco said.

"But we'll make sure they don't," Rand said.

"How are you going to do that?" Lauren asked. "You can't stay with us twenty-four hours a day. And next time they might bring four people instead of two, or even more."

"They were overconfident, attacking you in broad daylight," Rand said.

"They thought we'd be too frightened to fight back," Sophie said.

"They probably won't make that mistake again," Marco said. "But next time we'll be ready."

"What are you going to do?" Lauren asked.

"Right now, we're going back to your apartment and put these groceries away," Rand said. "You can change clothes and get something to eat, then we'll meet with the others at the captain's place. We'll come up with a plan of action there."

"What about my car?" Sophie asked.

"We'll send someone to get it later, and have them park it at a hotel or somewhere in town," Marco said. "That will confuse anyone looking for you."

"Why would Prentice want to kidnap me again?" Lauren asked when they were all in the truck. "He's already persuaded the grand jury not to believe me, and he's made me look like an idiot in the press."

"He must still feel you're a threat." Rand started the truck and headed out of the parking lot.

"You must know something that could incriminate him," Marco said. "Something you haven't revealed yet."

"I've told you and the police everything I know about him," she said. "Why would I hold back anything that could lock him away for good?"

"It would have to be something you don't even realize is important," Marco said. "But something that makes Prentice afraid enough to try to silence you, despite the risks."

"I don't believe he thinks there are any risks," Sophie said. "He's convinced he's invincible."

"People who believe that always end up making mistakes," Marco said.

"*Do* you know some secret about Prentice?" Sophie asked. "Something he'd kill to keep people from finding out?"

Lauren stared out the window, at the storefronts and apartment complexes and passing traffic. She didn't like to think of that dark time, when she'd been so lonely and afraid.

"I really wasn't with him that much," she said after a moment. "He kept me locked away— first in an upstairs bedroom, then in the mine. He would visit in the evenings several times a week. A few times we had dinner together. I tried to get him to talk about himself. I thought if I could figure out what made him tick, I could persuade him to let me go. But he evaded all my questions about his past, his childhood, his businesses—anything remotely personal."

"So what did you talk about?" Rand asked.

She sighed. "He spent most of his time trying to convince me to marry him."

"So he was romantic?" Rand's eyes met hers in the rearview mirror, clearly skeptical.

She made a face. "Not at all. His idea of a proposal was to persuade me of the benefits of marriage to him. I could have any material thing I wanted. He'd use his money and influence to buy me any job I aspired to. With his wealth and power and my beauty and ability to persuade the public, there was no limit to the changes we could make in government and society."

"He really said that?" Sophie asked. "About making changes to government and society?"

Lauren nodded. "I think he had this picture of me, installed as the anchor or host of some news show, reporting his ideas about unrestricted property rights and unregulated business and power for the privileged, and everyone seeing the brilliance of his ideas. He's fanatical enough to believe it could happen."

"So no romance." Was that relief she heard in Marco's voice?

"Not really. A few times he made an attempt to be, I guess you'd call it, 'warmer.'" She sat up straighter, a memory she'd pushed aside popping into her head. "One time he asked me to call him Bruno."

"Bruno?" Sophie laughed. "Where did he get that?"

"He said it could be my pet name for him." Lauren shook her head. "I guess that was his idea of romance."

"And he never tried anything physical?" Marco's voice was strained.

All she could see from her seat in the back of the truck was his neck, black hair neatly trimmed over his sun-bronzed skin. She studied the inch of tawny flesh exposed above his collar as she spoke. "He held my hand a couple of times and once he kissed me, but even the kiss was cold." Just thinking about kisses from Marco made her feel overheated.

"He's crazy." Sophie hugged her arms across her stomach. "And he scares me."

"It's easy to dismiss someone like him as

crazy," Marco said. "But he's operating according to some kind of internal logic, no matter how skewed. If we knew what that logic was, what really drives him, we would have a better chance of getting ahead of him and anticipating his next move."

"I had a lot of empty hours to spend trying to figure him out," Lauren said. "As far as I can tell, he believes he should be able to do whatever he wants, but I don't know why he believes that."

"He doesn't want the government telling him what he can and can't do with his property and his businesses," Rand said.

"Right," Lauren said. "But he doesn't believe that kind of freedom should extend to all people, only to ones like him, who already have money and position."

"Those who have, get more, and everybody else is out of luck," Rand said. "What kind of political philosophy is that?"

"I don't care about his politics," Marco said. "I only want to stop him from breaking the law."

"He's getting careless, attacking the girls in daylight, in a public place," Rand said. "We put more pressure on him, he's going to crack, and that's when we'll get him."

"I hope you're right," Lauren said. She didn't

want to live a life where she was scared to step out her door every morning.

"He knows you're stronger than him," Marco said. "That's why he's so desperate to silence you."

She didn't feel strong right now, but Marco's faith in her made her feel supported, as if, with his help, she could be strong again. "We'll stop him," she said. "With all of us fighting together, there's no way he can win."

THE MEETING AT Graham's that evening was like dozens of other meetings the Ranger team had held—everyone coming together to discuss a case and a strategy for solving it. But as Marco followed the others into the captain's living room, nothing felt the same as before. For one thing, they were all in civilian clothing—jeans and khakis and T-shirts or polos. Carmen wore a blouse with flowers, her long hair loose and earrings trimmed in crystals and feathers, reminding him that she was actually a pretty woman, not just a cop.

Women were the other big difference in this meeting. In addition to Carmen, Emma, Abby, Sophie and Lauren had joined them, ready to contribute what they knew about Richard Prentice, and their ideas for making a case against him. No longer was this about just what law enforcement could do. Though none of the Rangers had officially resigned their positions, they had taken temporary leaves or were using up accumulated vacation days in order to pursue this private investigation. If knowledge of their activities came to attention of their superiors, a number of them might very well lose their jobs.

"It feels strange, being here with all of you," Lauren said. She'd kept close to him all afternoon, her warm presence and soft scent reminding him of the biggest reason he was taking such a career risk. "Included, I mean."

"You probably know more about Prentice than anyone," Marco said. "You can help us find his weaknesses."

"I'm not sure he has any of those."

Graham stood before a whiteboard in front of his fireplace. To his right, Simon, who wore black jeans, a black snap-button Western shirt with large red roses and black lizard-skin cowboy boots, prepared to take notes. "The attack on Lauren and Sophie in the grocery store parking lot this afternoon was the rash move of a man who's not secure in his position," Graham said. "He's worried we're going to learn something he doesn't want anyone to know. He thinks Lauren could reveal that something."

"I've gone over everything I can remember

about my time at his ranch," Lauren said. "And I don't see anything incriminating. I never heard him talk about anything illegal. I never saw him do anything illegal. I never saw anything in his house that wasn't on display for everyone to see."

"Keep thinking," Graham said. "Maybe it will come to you. Meanwhile, we need to come up with a plan for uncovering everything possible about him."

"We've been over and over his background," Carmen said. "There just isn't a lot there. He was raised in Texas by a father who was a real estate attorney. His mother owned a dance studio. Prentice started out small, taking over failing oil companies and selling off their assets. A surge in oil prices made him a millionaire overnight and he began operating on a larger scale, amassing more money and influence. Some of his business decisions may have been unethical, but he's always operated just inside the law, at least in his business transactions."

"There's got to be something incriminating in his office," Lauren said.

"Why do you say that?" Michael asked from his seat on the couch beside Abby.

"Remember how he was shredding all those papers the night I was rescued?" she said. "But

Sophie and Rand chased him away before he'd gotten very far into the cabinet."

"He's been back to the house since," Rand said. "He's had plenty of time to destroy any evidence."

"Maybe not," she said. "Remember, he thinks he's invincible. And he kept those papers for a reason. He wouldn't want to destroy them unless it was absolutely necessary."

"I never understood why people would keep incriminating evidence—in writing—around," Emma said.

"Sometimes it's because they're so sure they'll never be caught," Graham said. "But sometimes it's because they need the evidence to hold over someone else."

"You mean—blackmail?" Emma asked.

"Something like that," Graham said.

"Who would Richard Prentice want to blackmail?" Sophie asked.

"Probably lots of people," Michael said. "But one person I can think of is Senator Mattheson. Maybe there's a reason the senator always dances to Prentice's tune."

"It would be interesting to know what Prentice has on Mattheson," Carmen agreed. "But proving blackmail could be tough."

"We won't know what he's hiding in those

filing cabinets until we get a closer look," Rand said.

"So we do what—break in?" Simon asked.

"Yes."

"Which makes anything we find inadmissible in court," Simon said.

"We don't take anything but photographs when we go in," Michael said. "But we find out what's there and we give the information to the local police."

"Who do nothing because Prentice has paid them off," Simon said.

"Then, we give it to the feds." Michael looked to Graham. "The FBI will have to act if we come up with convincing evidence."

Graham nodded. "How are we going to get in to look at the files? Prentice has at least two guards on shift at all times, plus surveillance cameras."

"I could go in."

The room fell silent. Marco couldn't believe what he'd heard. He stared at Lauren. She wore the determined expression he was coming to know well, jaw set, chin up, eyes flashing. He both loved the look and hated it, admiring her boldness yet wanting to protect her from danger. "I could do it," she said. "I could go there and tell him I want to talk about my feelings for him. He wouldn't refuse me, I'm sure. Once we're together, I could put knockout drops in his drink or something. I could search the file cabinets, and anything I saw would be admissible as evidence, right?"

"It's too dangerous," Marco said, before anyone else could speak.

"I've been there before and he didn't hurt me."

"Are you forgetting the package he sent? The death threat? The attack this afternoon?" His voice rose, and he tried to rein in the emotions that made him want to seize her and hustle her out of the room until she came to her senses.

She swallowed. "I haven't forgotten those things. But this is our best chance to get close to him and get the evidence we need."

"I won't let you do it," he said.

"This isn't your decision to make." Her eyes met his, troubled but determined.

"No, but it's mine," Graham said. "I can't let a civilian take that kind of risk."

She stood, steady on her feet, and faced the ranks of officers and friends who sat around the living room. "Let me do this," she said. "If I don't, I won't be able to walk out my door without worrying about someone attacking me. I won't be able to get a job without some new rumor about my sanity popping up." Her gaze came to rest on Marco, silently asking for understanding. "I know you all have a lot at stake here, and that it's important to make your case. But my life is on the line here—not because I'll be in danger if I go to Richard's ranch, but because I won't have a life worth living if I don't."

He stood and moved beside her. He wanted to wrap his arms around her and never let her go, to tell her she was brave and foolish and too precious for him to lose. But he didn't touch her. "If you do this, let me go with you," he said.

"Richard would never permit it," she said. "He knows you're with the Rangers. If you show up with me, he'll be instantly suspicious."

"He'll know one Ranger will be no match for all his guards, and he'll be curious enough to want to hear what you have to say to let you in, in spite of my presence."

"He might kill you."

"He could kill you, too." His throat constricted around the words. "Are you afraid?"

"Terrified. But I'm more afraid of sitting here and doing nothing."

He took her hand and squeezed it.

"I'm telling you not to do this," Graham said, with the air of a man choosing his words carefully. "But as of four o'clock this afternoon, I'm not your commanding officer anymore."

"I'm just a rogue agent, acting on my own," Marco said. "I understand."

"I'll provide backup." Rand stood.

"We all will." Michael stood also, and then they were all on their feet, men and women alike. They began talking about the steps they'd need to take, equipment they'd need to acquire, when the best time would be to approach Prentice, how they could keep him off guard.

Lauren squeezed Marco's hand and moved closer. "Thank you," she whispered.

He slid his hand under her hair to caress the back of her neck. "You're either the bravest woman I know, or the craziest," he said.

"I think it's a little of both." She looked up at him. "Is that all right?"

"It's more than all right." He wanted to kiss her, but not now. Not with all these people watching. He'd save that moment for later, when he could show her, without words, all she was coming to mean to him.

Chapter Ten

Lauren felt as if her safety belt was the only thing keeping her from levitating in her seat. Nervous energy jittered through her, making her hyperaware of everything around her—the brilliant gold and purple of wildflowers on the side of the road, the smoothness of the leather seat against her bare arm, the subtle spice-and-soap scent of Marco in the driver's seat, the way the muscles of his forearm bunched as he gripped the steering wheel.

Was this nerves or the beginning of a manic episode? She'd taken her medication, done her breathing exercises, sent up prayers. How did so-called normal people—people without this anomaly in their brains or chemical imbalance or whatever you wanted to call it—act in a bizarre situation like this? She had no idea. All she could do was trust her own instincts—and the man beside her—and hope they didn't lead her astray.

"How are you doing?" Marco asked.

She smoothed her hands down her thighs, trying to dry her sweating palms. "I'll be okay," she said. She plucked a loose thread from the fabric. She'd chosen the outfit carefully, opting for a short skirt instead of slacks, hoping to tempt Prentice with a little sexiness, but selecting flat sandals instead of heels in case she had to run. She fought the urge to laugh, afraid if she started she'd be that much closer to hysteria. Who would have thought she'd ever be debating fashion choices for becoming a potential hostage—or murder victim?

Marco turned his Jeep into the gravel drive that crossed Prentice's ranch and stopped at the gate. A guard emerged from the stone guardhouse and Lauren gasped.

"Something wrong?" Marco asked.

She shook her head. "I know him. His name is Henry." He'd been one of the nicer men who'd guarded her, polite and respectful, unlike the men who'd tried to grope her or treated her with disdain.

"This is private property," Henry said as soon as Marco lowered the driver's side window. "You need to turn around."

"Hello, Henry." Lauren leaned forward so he could get a good look at her. "I need to talk to Richard."

He blinked, clearly thrown off guard, but he recovered quickly. "Hello, Ms. Starling. Do you have an appointment?"

"No, but I think he'll want to see me, don't you?" She gave him her brightest smile, the one she used for pageants and other public appearances. The one that had graced billboards and even the sides of buses all over Denver when she'd been the star of Metro News.

Henry shifted his gaze to Marco. "What's he doing here?"

"Richard has his bodyguards. I decided I needed one, too." She'd lobbied for this frank approach, sure Prentice would see through a lie.

"Wait here." He stepped inside the guardhouse and pulled out his phone.

"He's not going to like my being here," Marco said, keeping his voice low.

"No, but Richard is very big on cost-benefit analysis. The cost of having you along won't outweigh the benefit of seeing me." She was hoping that was true, anyway. If Richard was the one behind the attacks on her, he wouldn't pass up the opportunity to have her where he would think he could easily control her.

Henry returned. "Step out of the car, sir," he ordered. "I need to search you."

Marco stood with arms outstretched and

allowed Henry to frisk him. The guard stopped at Marco's ankle, pulled up the leg of his jeans and extracted a small pistol from the holster there. Lauren felt faint; she hadn't even known Marco was armed. "You can pick this up on your way out," Henry said. "Mr. Prentice doesn't allow weapons in the house. I'll also need your phone." He turned to Lauren. "Yours, too, Ms. Starling."

"My phone?" She clutched at her purse, which contained her smartphone.

"New rules." The guard held out his hand. "All visitors must surrender their phones. I'll return it to you when you leave."

She sent a panicked look to Marco. Having a gun wouldn't have made her feel safer, but being without her phone meant being completely cut off from the outside world.

Marco pulled his own phone from his pocket and handed it to the guard. Hand shaking, she did the same.

"Why did they take our phones?" she whispered when Marco rejoined her in the car.

"Another way for Prentice to remind us he's in charge."

She glanced at the guard, who'd carried their phones and Marco's pistol into the stone guardhouse. "What were you going to do with that gun?" she asked.

"Whatever I had to." He put the Jeep in gear and they followed a second guard down the drive and up to the fake castle Prentice called home.

"He told me this place was designed to look like a famous castle in Germany," she said.

"So he made it this ugly on purpose."

Another guard met them at the front door and escorted them to the library. Marco studied the bookshelves. "Do you think he ever reads any of these?" he asked. "Or are they just for show?"

"I think he told me he likes to read history."

"So you are remembering more things he told you?"

"Yes, but nothing significant, only trivia."

The door opened and Prentice entered. He was dressed casually, for him, a sport coat replacing his usual suit jacket, his shirt open at the collar, with no tie. "Lauren, dear, how lovely to see you." He kissed her cheek and squeezed her arm—too hard, but she forced herself not to flinch, or to show any reaction to him but pleasure.

"It's good to see you, too, Richard," she lied.

He ignored Marco, not even glancing in his direction, and led Lauren to a sofa by the cold fireplace. He sat, pulling her down beside him. "I knew you'd be back," he said.

"You did?"

"Of course. I knew you'd realize we're meant to be together."

She couldn't decide if he really believed this, or if he was saying it to get a rise out of Marco, who had followed them across the room and sat opposite them, stone-faced. "This is my friend Marco," she said. "I don't know if you two have met."

"I know all about the Ranger." His tone was dismissive. "What can I do for you?"

"I'd love something to drink," she said. "Maybe some coffee?" She had knockout drops in a vial tucked into her sleeve—like some movie spy. Carmen had assured her they were potent enough to down a linebacker.

"Certainly." He picked up the phone on the table beside the sofa. "Please bring Ms. Starling a cup of coffee. One sugar, no cream."

"Aren't you going to join me?" she asked.

"No." Again the dismissive tone.

What now? She had to get Richard out of the way so that she could search his office, down the hall.

"What did you want to talk to me about?" he asked.

Right. They had to talk. The Rangers had drilled her on what they thought she should say to him—meaningless small talk that amounted to verbal stalling. But she decided to take another approach. "I was very hurt by the things you said about me in the papers," she told him.

He sat back, one arm stretched along the top of the sofa, just behind her head. "What things?"

"That I'm crazy. That I'm a liar."

A man arrived with her coffee, and they fell silent until they were alone once more.

"Now, Lauren, I never called you a liar," Richard chided. "I merely felt you gave the press and police an unfair picture of our relationship."

The man really was delusional. "Richard, you kept me a prisoner." Marco stared at her, clearly warning her to be more cautious, but she'd set aside all caution when she agreed to come here. She might as well try to find out what Prentice was thinking.

"I was keeping you safe," Richard said. "When you came to me, I was concerned you might hurt yourself. You needed someone to look after you."

"I'm an adult. I'm fully capable of looking after myself." She picked up the coffee cup, wanting something to do with her hands, to hide her growing agitation, but then she set it down again. She didn't trust Richard not to have put something in the drink.

"Are you really capable of taking care of yourself?" Richard asked. "Then, why did you bring him along?" He glared at Marco, who returned the angry look.

"I brought him because the last time I came here alone, you wouldn't let me leave," she said.

"You were free to go anytime you wanted," he said. "All you had to do was ask."

"I asked." Repeatedly. She'd also tried demanding, crying, running away and fighting. Each time he'd had her restrained, carried away and locked in a room.

He smiled an oily, patronizing look. "You didn't ask," he said. "You begged to stay."

She opened her mouth to argue with him, but the slight shake of Marco's head caught her attention. Right. Don't argue. Go along with him. "I'm trying to rebuild my reputation now," she said. "I'm hoping you can help."

"I've always tried to help you before," he said. "But if we're going to talk about hurt feelings, I'm wounded that you feel you need protection from me."

She leaned toward him. She was taking a lot of risks coming here today; why not take one more? "I had to bring Marco because someone is trying to hurt me," she said. "My car was tampered with, and yesterday I was attacked by two men in the parking lot of a grocery store."

He furrowed his brow, the picture of concern. "That is worrying. But are you sure it was an attack? Maybe they were merely fans who wanted your autograph."

"They were not fans, and they didn't ask for autographs."

"Why would someone attack you?" he asked.

"You tell me. Did you have anything to do with those attacks?"

His expression remained as impassive as ever, not even a glimmer of guilt or concern in his eyes. "I imagine a woman like you would have made many enemies in your life," he said.

"A woman like me?" The way he said the words made the hair stand up at the back of her neck.

"You're beautiful, but unreliable." He moved his hand to cradle the back of her head. "Prone to irrational behavior."

The only thing irrational about her now was the fear that gripped her at his touch. She bit the inside of her cheek to keep from screaming as he rubbed his thumb back and forth across the side of her neck. Across from them, Marco stiffened and leaned forward as if ready to spring up.

"If I'm so irrational, then what do you see in me?" she asked. "How would I ever fit into your life?"

"That would be the beauty of our alliance." He continued stroking, and slid closer, his thigh touching hers. "I could rebuild your reputation. Money and power are transformative. It no longer matters what you did or who you were. All that is important is who people think you are. Build the right image and you can do anything."

"That's what you've done for yourself," she said. "You've built an image, and now you think you can do anything."

"I *can* do anything." His fingers closed around her neck, hard enough that she cried out.

"Let go!" she cried. "You're hurting me."

"Sometimes we hurt the ones we love," he said, increasing the pressure of his fingers.

Her heart pounded painfully and she had trouble breathing. She clawed at him, but he leaned over her, holding her down with surprising force. "Marco!" she cried.

"He can't save you now," Prentice growled. "Don't come any closer, Ranger, or I'll kill her." His hand tightened even more around her neck and her vision clouded. Was he trying to choke her, or to break her neck? She beat her fists against him with no effect. And she was growing weaker…

A weight crushed her, squeezing breath and

life from her. Above her, Prentice struggled with someone. Marco? She fought to remain conscious and was dimly aware of the two men grappling on top of her.

Then the pressure released and a strong hand grasped hers and pulled her up. "Come on," Marco said. "We've got to get to the study before the guards show up."

THEY LEFT PRENTICE lying in a heap on the library floor. Not dead, but knocked out from the blow Marco had landed on his chin. "Wh-what happened?" Lauren asked as she stumbled from the room after Marco. "What about Richard?"

"He's out for now. He's lucky I didn't tear him in two." The sight of the billionaire's hands on her had filled him with rage.

"He was going to kill me," she said, half sobbing now. "Right there in front of you."

"He was arrogant enough to think so," Marco said. "But I never would have let it happen." He pulled her up beside him and put his arm around her. "You're safe now. Come on. We have to get to work."

The door to Prentice's office stood open. Clearly, he felt secure in his own home. "You look through the filing cabinet. I'll search the desk," Marco said.

Though Prentice could have afforded the sleekest designer furnishings, he chose to work at an old-fashioned wooden desk, the top easily five feet across, the mahogany finish scarred and worn. Marco rifled through the drawers, passing over the office supplies, peppermints and scattered sticky notes with cryptic messages: "Talk to JR about Wednesday." He pocketed a few of these, then turned his attention to the file drawer at the lower right-hand side of the desk. It contained stacks of neatly folded blueprints and land surveys, along with brochures for developments he assumed Prentice had an interest in.

"There's just files with names of companies he owns or has an interest in," Lauren said. She stood before the filing cabinet, the top drawer open.

"Don't bother reading through things," he said. "Take anything of interest."

He stood back and studied the desk. Why would a man like Prentice, whose house was furnished in either fine antiques or the latest styles, opt for a desk that looked better suited for the junkyard?

He knelt and began feeling along the underside and backs of all the drawers. Sure enough, behind the top left-hand drawer he felt an indentation, and a hidden spring. When he pressed it, a small wooden box dropped into his hand.

He moved into the light to examine the contents of the hidden compartment. A man in a military uniform stared up at him, from a black-and-white photo as worn and faded with age as the desk. The man in the picture had removed his cap and wore his hair slicked down and parted sharply on one side, a thin moustache above his tightly compressed lips. Why would Prentice hide this? He tucked it into his shirt.

"I may have something." Lauren ran to him, a slip of paper in her hand.

He examined the three numbers written on the paper: 96-14-6. "Is it a date? June 14, 1996?" he asked.

"I think it's a combination," she said. "Maybe for a safe?"

"Then we need to find the safe."

He opened the closet and found nothing but an overcoat and a set of golf clubs. Judging by the dust that covered them, Prentice hadn't played in a while. "I've found it!" Lauren called.

She'd removed a picture above a credenza on the back wall of the office to reveal the slightly recessed door of a safe. "Hurry and open it," he said.

While she spun the dial, he moved to the door and listened. No sign of the guards yet, but he was sure it was only a matter of time before they showed up. Too bad that desk hadn't contained a gun. He looked around for a weapon and had to settle for a letter opener. It looked flimsy and would be no match for the automatic weapons the guards usually carried.

"It's open," Lauren called, and he rejoined her in front of the safe. She reached in and pulled out handfuls of paper and gave him half.

"These look like deeds to property," she said as she flipped through her stack of documents.

"Mine, too," he said. He stopped at one yellowed square of paper. "And Richard Prentice's birth certificate. And a passport." That would prove interesting reading later.

"Did you hear something?" She looked toward the door, all color draining from her face. A sound like a slamming door, then the pounding of running feet echoed along the hallway.

"We have to get out of here." Marco stuffed his pockets with the passport and other papers. Lauren did the same with her handful of documents.

"Which way do we go?" she asked.

"This way." He took her hand and pulled her toward the room's only window. But when he yanked on the sash, it wouldn't budge. He felt along the frame for a locking mechanism.

"Maybe it's nailed shut," she said.

The footsteps in the hallway drew closer, and now they could hear shouting. "Search the house! Don't let them get away!"

"Stand back," Marco said, and picked up the heavy, rolling chair from behind the desk. He heaved it through the window, the frame shattering and glass exploding with the impact. An alarm began to wail, the deafening Klaxon shrieking right above their heads. A guard burst into the room and gunfire splintered the wood beside Marco's head.

"Come on!" he yelled, and shoved Lauren in front of him out the window, then dived after her in a shower of glass and splinters and flying bullets.

Chapter Eleven

Instincts honed from years of training kicked in as Marco turned to face the two guards who appeared at the window. He had to buy time for Lauren to get out of range of their guns, but he had no weapon of his own.

Correct that—he had no firearm. But he had a quick mind and an agile body, two powerful weapons he could use to his advantage against foes who were certain of the superiority provided by all their hardware.

He dived to one side, out of sight of the guards. "Run!" he urged Lauren. "As fast and as far as you can."

"But I can't leave you," she protested, her face contorted with anxiety.

"I'll catch up with you, I promise. Go!"

She hesitated only a moment more before turning and racing away, her feet pounding over the rough ground. The guards began firing after her, bullets striking the ground with small thuds, little volcano eruptions of dirt marking the spot where each one hit.

One of the guards leaned out of the window, bracing his weapon against the frame for a steadier shot. Marco scooped a rock from the ground at his feet and fired it, a ninety-mile-per-hour fastball to the side of the man's head. It struck with all the force of a missile, dropping the guard to his knees, blood trickling down the side of his head.

The second guard turned and located Marco, aiming point-blank. No way would he miss at this close range. Marco dived sideways and rolled, the bullet whistling past him. He sprang to his feet and ran, dodging and weaving, presenting as difficult a target as possible. He raced toward the sun, forcing the shooter to aim into the glare, and he wove behind piles of boulders and the gnarled trunks of piñons whenever possible. The guard's fire became less and less accurate, until Marco was out of range. He began looking for Lauren.

"Marco! Over here!"

He stopped, and turned to look behind him. She was crouched in the narrow space between a group of scrubby post oak trees and a rounded gray boulder, its surface painted with green, yellow and red lichen. The deep shadows of her hiding place almost completely hid her from view, though as Marco approached, she emerged farther, sunlight gilding her pale blond hair.

"Are you all right?" he asked as he drew nearer.

"Terrified, but I'll be okay. What about you?" She swept her gaze over him, brow knitted.

"I'm good." Better than good. If not for the danger to her, he might have exulted in this feeling of power and strength. The past weeks of the necessary tedium of an investigation had left him feeling dull and slow. Their encounter with the guards had sharpened his senses and summoned all the warrior skills around which he'd shaped his life.

He took her arm and helped her the rest of the way out of her hiding place. "We have to keep moving," he said. "They'll be looking for us."

"Moving where?" she asked, even as she hurried to keep up with the brisk pace he set.

"We need to get to the road. From there we can get to town, or flag down someone with a phone who can help us."

"Which way is the road?"

The landscape around them provided no landmarks, only miles of sun-parched grasses and stunted trees, rocky boulders and the distant green line that marked the canyon, and beyond that the snowcapped peaks of the mountains. "The road is that direction." Marco pointed toward the southwest. "If we keep the sun at our backs, we'll be fine."

"I guess this is the kind of thing they teach in Special Forces," she said as they corrected their course to head east.

"Boy Scouts."

She laughed. "You never struck me as the Boy Scout type."

"A church came into the projects when I was nine and started up a troop. I spent two weeks at camp that summer, learning all about trail finding and stuff. But the next year I guess the church decided it wasn't worth it or they couldn't get volunteers or something. They didn't come back."

"But you liked it? The trail finding and stuff?"

"Yeah." He'd felt at home in the wilderness, in a way he never had on the streets of East LA. He didn't have to play the tough-guy role or play up to people he didn't like, or be afraid when he was on his own in the wild. He could rely on himself and his own skills out there, in a way he'd seldom been able to rely on other people.

He took Lauren's hand. "It's going to be

all right," he said. "I know what I'm doing out here."

"I know you do." She squeezed his fingers. "That's why I'm not nearly as afraid as I would be if I was by myself."

"You'd do okay," he said. "You're a survivor."

She laughed again, a more derisive sound this time. "I don't know how you can say that. You haven't exactly seen me at my best."

"You survived six weeks as Prentice's prisoner. You didn't let that defeat you. And you haven't let bipolar disorder defeat you."

"Okay, so I guess I am mentally pretty strong. But that doesn't mean I have the know-how or physical strength to survive out here."

"Well, you don't have to worry. I'll be strong for both of us."

She smiled and leaned into him, in a kind of half hug that made him feel ten feet tall and invincible, but also more vulnerable than he had since he was a small boy. But being vulnerable didn't frighten him when he was with her. Not anymore. He guessed that meant he'd learned to trust her—to trust what he could be with her.

He looked around at the open, roadless prairie. The Jeeps Prentice's guards used could easily travel across country, and in this terrain two people on foot would be visible from a long way off. "We need to find cover," he said. "A draw or creek bed or somewhere we can travel without being so visible." He pointed toward a line of trees about a quarter mile to the north. "Let's try there."

Her sandals, though flat, weren't made for travel in this rough country, not like his hiking boots. But she kept going, grim faced and limping at times. He pretended not to notice. No need to make her feel she was less in his eyes, especially since the opposite was true. He admired her determination more with each step.

Years of runoff from spring snowmelt had cut a narrow ravine through the landscape, choked with scrub oak and tough grasses. The red-brown dirt crumbled as they half slid, half climbed into the depression. Marco put his arm around Lauren's waist to steady her and she leaned into him, breathing heavily. "Do you really think they won't see us here?" she asked.

"We'll be less visible here than in the open." He took her hand and led her through the maze of brush, over rocks and around clumps of cactus. They hadn't traveled more than a few hundred yards when a low, mechanical whine cut the desert silence.

Lauren froze, head up, alert. "Someone's coming," she whispered.

He nodded. The noise grew more distinct—the rumble of an engine in low gear and the popping of tires on gravel. "Just one vehicle, I think," he said. "Headed this way."

"Can they see us?" She looked around at the stunted trees and grasses closing in on all sides.

"They might have seen us headed this way," he said. They probably had; why else would the Jeep head so deliberately in that direction? "But they won't have known where we disappeared to." At least, they wouldn't unless they knew the country very well. He doubted the kind of muscle Prentice favored had spent much of their free time exploring the backcountry wilderness, and their regular duties kept them close to Prentice's mansion. He took Lauren's hand again. "Let's find a place where we can keep an eye on them."

He led the way along the bottom of the ravine until he spotted a side channel cutting the bank, a dense knot of wild plum trees anchoring the spot. They climbed the bank and settled among the close trunks of the plums. He would have liked a pair of binoculars, but even without them he could see the Jeep, a cloud of dust marking its approach.

As it drew nearer, he identified two guards. The man in the passenger seat held a semiautomatic rifle, the stock balanced on his thigh, the barrel pointed upward. He wondered if the man's orders were to bring them in alive—or to shoot them and leave their bodies for the coyotes and other wild animals to scatter.

Lauren pressed up against his back, looking over his shoulder, her mouth next to his ear. "Do you think they see us?" she whispered.

Her warm breath tickled his ear, and when he breathed in he smelled the floral-spice aroma of her perfume, underlaid with the scent of feminine sweat and the sage leaves crushed beneath their feet. Every nerve in his body responded to the feel of her against him—the curve of her breasts pressed against his back, her hip bone against the back of his thigh, her warmth seeping into him. He reached back to caress her side. "They can't see us," he said softly. "They won't see us." But if they did, if they got out of the Jeep and came toward them, he would fight with everything he had to protect her.

The Jeep reached the edge of the ravine and stopped, a few hundred yards south of their hiding spot, at about the place where they'd descended into the depression. The guard in the driver's seat scanned the area with a pair of binoculars, skimming over the grouping of plum trees with no hesitation. He thought Lauren had stopped breathing, her heart hammering against him.

The driver lowered the binoculars and put the Jeep into gear once more and drove on, past their hiding spot, until only a diminishing trail of white dust marked its path.

Lauren sagged against him, her face pressed against his back. "I was so scared," she whispered. He felt her fear as much as heard it in her voice. She trembled against him, and he wondered how close she was to breaking down. She'd been through so much. How long before it all became too much for her to take?

He turned and gathered her close, pulling her tight against him. She wrapped her arms around him and returned the embrace, and when she raised her head to look at him, he didn't hesitate, but kissed her.

LAUREN DIDN'T KNOW how much she'd wanted that kiss until Marco's lips covered hers. She wanted it the way famished people want food or thirsty travelers need water. That kiss reminded her of things that were more important than Prentice and his guards, reasons she would keep going, better things to come on the other side of the terror and worry and fear.

His lips caressed hers, soft but firm, as his hands smoothed along the sides of her body, holding her steady, reassuring her that he appreciated everything he touched. He adjusted the angle of his head and ran his tongue across the seam of her lips, and she opened to him, eager to taste, to give of herself more fully. She arched to him, the hard planes of his chest sending a thrill through her, reminding her of his strength, of the power of his masculinity. She clutched at his back, wanting to be nearer still, to lose herself in the moment.

He pulled away gently, keeping his arms around her, his gaze fixed on her. She blinked up at him, a little dazed, and struggled to regain her composure. Doubt swept in to replace the confidence with which she'd welcomed his embrace. "Were you just trying to take my mind off my fear?" she asked.

"I wanted to kiss you." He brushed her hair back from her forehead, a tender gesture that sent a new surge of desire through her. "I've been wanting to kiss you for a while."

She wanted to answer him with another kiss, but told herself she shouldn't get carried away in the moment. She needed to play it cool until she was more sure of him, sure of them. "And you thought now was an appropriate time?"

Amusement danced in his eyes and tugged the corners of his mouth upward, almost into a smile. "Sometimes it's good to listen to your instincts."

"I like your instincts." She smoothed her hands up his chest to his shoulders, savoring the attraction, drawing out the moment.

But instead of another kiss, he stepped back and released his hold on her. "If we were somewhere else, somewhere more comfortable, safer, I'd like to continue this conversation, but we need to move on before those two come back."

The fear surged forward again, but not as overwhelming this time, diminished by the strength of these feelings between them— feelings she was in no hurry to try to define. "What do we do now?" she asked. "I mean, about getting away."

"We keep going." He nodded ahead of them, indicating the trail through the narrow ravine.

"Aren't we traveling away from the road?"

"For now. If the ravine doesn't curve east soon, we'll look for another route. It's more important to stay out of sight of the searchers."

She fell into step behind him, content to let him choose the path through the choking brush that scratched her bare legs and caught at her sandals. "Richard is probably furious," she said after a while.

"Good. Emotional people are more apt to make mistakes in judgment."

Was he saying that their own judgment might be clouded by the emotions they felt for each other? With his back to her, she couldn't gauge his meaning by the expression on his face. Not that Mr. Inscrutable ever gave her many clues as to what was going on in his head or his heart. "Did they teach you that in Special Forces?" she asked.

"Yes."

"So soldiers aren't supposed to have emotions."

"You learn to sublimate them. To set them aside until a more appropriate time to process them."

"What if an appropriate time never comes?"

"Then, you end up with things you haven't dealt with."

"Do you have things you haven't dealt with?"

"Yes."

She hadn't expected this frankness from a man who was so skilled at remaining cool and somehow outside every fray. The knowledge that he trusted her with even this small confession of weakness moved her. "Maybe you'll tell me sometime," she said.

He stepped over a log, the remains of an ancient lightning-scarred tree, and turned to help her over, as well. But he didn't release her hand right away. Instead, he squeezed her fingers. "Maybe I will."

She smiled to herself as he turned to lead the way once more and she felt stronger and more confident as they traveled in silence for another half mile or so, when the ravine turned east, and so did they. She let her thoughts drift, content to follow Marco and not think too much about where they were headed or why. As long as he was in charge, everything was all right. Prentice had money and manpower, but Marco had brains and skills.

And she had Marco. For now, that seemed more than enough.

He put out a hand to stop her. She stumbled a little and he caught her. "What is it?" she asked. "Is something wrong?"

"There's water up ahead. It's just a puddle, but it will help us keep going."

At the mention of water, she let out a low moan. She'd been trying not to think about how thirsty she was. She looked around him at the muddy puddle about two feet across, the water the color of milk chocolate. She tried to swallow. "We're going to drink that?"

"We'll strain it first." He reached up and tugged at his sleeve until it tore. Pulling harder, he ripped the fabric at the seams, then knelt beside the puddle. "It would be better if we had some kind of container, but we may have to soak the cloth in the water, then squeeze it into our mouths. It might taste a little muddy, but it should be all right."

She nodded, telling herself she shouldn't

be squeamish. This wasn't about taste or hygiene—they were trying to stay alive.

She started to step back to give him more room to work when movement out of the corner of her eye made her freeze. The ground just to her right undulated, then what had at first appeared to be a smear of mud and dried leaves shifted and became the coil of a snake. She gasped and made a choking noise, incoherent with fear.

"What is it?" Marco, still kneeling beside the puddle, looked over his shoulder at her. He glanced at her face, then followed her horrified gaze toward the ground.

The snake raised its head, weaving slightly, tongue flickering, menace in every movement. Its tail vibrated, a castanet clatter of warning. "Is that—?" Lauren couldn't finish the sentence.

"A rattlesnake," Marco said.

Chapter Twelve

Marco stared at the snake, the mottled brown-and-tan coils seeming to emerge from the earth like a mythological beast, born of mud and rotting matter and menace. He tried to swallow, dry mouthed, and struggled to breathe evenly through his nose, to slow his racing heart. He was smart enough to be afraid of many things—enemies with guns, for instance. But some fears went beyond rationality to something more innate and primitive. Chief among these was the fear of snakes. No matter that Michael Dance had assured them that the native prairie rattlers found in the park were much less lethal than their cousins to the south and west—a rattlesnake was a rattlesnake, venomous and terrifying.

All this time he'd been so focused on Richard Prentice and his men, he'd forgotten that they weren't the only enemies he and Lauren had to worry about out here in the wilderness.

The snake flicked its tongue and coiled tighter, ready to strike. Lauren's calf was in striking distance. She stared at the viper, mesmerized, her face drained of color. Marco searched the ground for a rock or a stout stick to use as a weapon, but found nothing.

A memory came to him of a television show he and Rand had watched one evening about snake hunters in the Amazon, who had killed venomous snakes with their bare hands. He and Rand had joked that they preferred using a pistol, but he didn't have a pistol now. Time to try the snake hunters' method, but he'd only have one chance.

He pulled his key ring from his pocket and tossed it so that it landed about a foot to the snake's right. At the metallic chink on the rocks, the snake swiveled its head away from Lauren. Marco lunged and grabbed the snake by the tail. It was like picking up a heavy garden hose, one pulsing with flowing water. Lauren screamed as he whipped the snake into the trunk of the nearest tree. He released it and jumped back, then stood, breathing hard and staring at the limp body of the predator.

"Is it dead?" Lauren asked from behind him.

"It's not after us anymore," he said. "That's all that matters."

She moved into his arms and rested her head

on his shoulder. "I don't think I've ever been so terrified," she said. "It was worse than facing Prentice and his guards, or those men in the parking lot who tried to kidnap me and Sophie."

"There's something about snakes," he said, rubbing his hand up and down her back. The contact calmed him, too. "I think it's a primitive fear, hardwired into our DNA."

She raised her head to study him. "I didn't think you were afraid of anything."

"I'm a man, not a robot."

She smiled. "Good to hear you admit it."

He started to ask what she meant by that, then thought better of it. He'd spent years learning to hide his feelings from others. Maybe he'd gotten a little too proficient at that particular skill.

Cautious, keeping a look out for more predators, they knelt and drank from the muddy water, straining it through Marco's shirt. It wasn't very refreshing, but it would keep them going a little while longer.

They moved on, making a wide berth around the inert snake, and resumed their trek toward the road. The water had revived them, and maybe the promise of safety soon added energy and purpose to their steps. They'd been traveling an hour or so when the sound of a car made them stop once more. Marco listened, then said, "It's traveling faster. I think we're near the road."

LAUREN'S HEARTBEAT SPED up at his words, hope forming a knot in her throat. The road meant safety and eventual rescue. They began walking again, faster. If the rough terrain would have allowed it, she would have broken into a run.

Another hundred yards along, she saw a bridge up ahead where a paved road crossed over the ravine, which widened and flattened, its sides mostly cleared of vegetation. She started toward this clearing, but Marco pulled her back. "Wait," he said.

Forcing herself to keep still, she waited. Half a minute passed, and then she heard a vehicle approaching. When the familiar Jeep appeared, she stifled a groan. She waited for the vehicle to pass before she whispered, "They're still looking for us."

"They won't give up," he said. "Not until they have to. There's too much at stake."

There was too much at stake for her and Marco if Prentice's men found them, too. She started to ask him if he had a plan B when yet another vehicle approached. This proved to also be a Jeep with two burly men in camouflage fatigues. Five minutes later, a third Jeep passed.

"I didn't know Prentice had that many guards," she said, the whine of the third Jeep's engine fading in the distance.

"He probably called in extra manpower."

"What are we going to do?"

"They're never all in the same area at once. We can time them, find a window of opportunity when we can evade them."

He made it sound so logical. So easy. "We can do that?"

He nodded. "But it will be better if we wait until dark. That will make it easier."

The thought of waiting here, in the heat and dust and cacti, for several more hours until evening made her feel almost too tired to stand. She took his hand again, drawing strength from his calm assurance. "Where do we wait?"

He led her back down the draw, to a place where erosion had undercut the bank of the ravine to form a shaded hollow. He sat and she settled beside him, his arm around her shoulder. She tried to ignore the rock digging into the small of her back, or the thirst that made her lips feel swollen. "I'm still trying to picture you as a Boy Scout," she said.

"We didn't have uniforms or anything. Not really. I think I had one of those little scarf things."

"A kerchief?" She smiled at this image of him as a ragtag little boy in a yellow Scouting neck cloth.

"Were you a Girl Scout?" he asked.

"Oh, no. Girl Scouts weren't cool, and I was always cool."

"I'll bet you were always the most popular girl. And the prettiest one."

"I was. Does that sound terribly vain?" She shook her head ruefully. "I was awful. Selfish. I sometimes wonder if all the bad stuff that has happened as an adult is because I was so terrible and insensitive when I was growing up."

"You were a kid. Kids act out. Sometimes they're insensitive. Besides, I don't believe in that stuff."

"In what stuff?"

"Karma, or whatever you want to call it. We don't get what we deserve in life. If that was true, then little kids would never die of cancer and men like Prentice wouldn't be rich and powerful." He squeezed her shoulder. "You can't change what you did before, so don't beat yourself up over it."

"You're right. So instead of moaning about the past, let's think about the future. Do you think there's anything useful in those papers we took from Richard's study?"

"Why don't we take a look and see?" He

shifted and pulled a sheaf of papers from inside his shirt. She withdrew her own collection of documents from her pockets and they spread the papers on the dirt in front of them: a picture, a birth certificate, a passport and what looked like deeds.

She picked up the picture and studied it. "This looks old," she said. The photograph was black-and-white, with a narrow white border all around. The man in it stared sternly ahead, his hair slicked to his scalp, his moustache two smudges above his thin upper lip. "Maybe from the 1940s. That could be a military uniform he's wearing."

"There's writing on the back," Marco said. "What does it say?"

She flipped the picture over. The ink was faded to a pale blue, the looping letters indecipherable. "I don't think it's English," she said. "I can't make it out. Except the name. Bruno Adel." She frowned. "Bruno was the name Richard asked me to call him, but this clearly isn't him."

"Maybe it's a relative," Marco said. He picked up the passport and flipped through it. "He made a lot of trips to Venezuela."

"That's because he was dating a model there. The ambassador's daughter."

"These stamps go back almost ten years.

I don't think they would have been dating that long."

"I doubt it. I don't think she was that old."

He tapped the passport against his palm. "So maybe he had another reason for going there so often."

"Maybe he has a business there? He supposedly has property all over the world."

They turned their attention to the deeds. She shuffled through the half dozen pieces of paper, then handed them to Marco. "Nothing here looks familiar to me," she said. "And there are just addresses, not names."

Marco held out one of the deeds. "This one. I think the address is for a house in Denver where a bunch of illegal immigrants were held. I think I remember it from the court documents. And there's another address in Denver—that could be a house we busted as the center of a sex trafficking ring."

"So those are things that could help you make a case against Richard?"

"Maybe." He scanned the papers again. "The deeds are in the name of RP Holdings, Inc."

"Richard Prentice Holdings?"

"Or he might say these businesses have nothing to do with him."

"Then, why was he keeping these papers in his safe?"

"We've already seen how good he is at explaining away evidence." Marco laid the papers back on the pile in front of them. "Good enough to persuade the grand jury."

"But he never appeared before the grand jury," she said. "That isn't allowed."

"He didn't have to testify himself. He used his influence and money behind the scenes to shape the testimonies of the experts who did testify." Marco looked scornful. "Of course, we'll never prove it, but I'm sure that's what happened."

"Then, what we need is something that will undermine his credibility," she said. "The way he's tried to undermine mine." If only Prentice had a history of mental illness, or a criminal record, or anything that would make him look like the lowlife he really was.

Marco folded the papers and tucked them back in his shirt. "Try not to worry about it now. Get some rest. You want to be alert when we make a break for it tonight."

"Will you rest, too?" she asked.

He pulled her down so that she reclined against him, her head nestled in the hollow of his shoulder. "I'll keep watch," he said. "I won't let anything happen to you."

It was absurd, she thought as she closed her eyes, to believe that one man could keep a half a dozen or more guards with guns at bay, that he could stop a murderer who wanted them both dead. But Marco made her believe that she could trust him with anything—with her life. Even with her heart.

MARCO HAD BEEN determined not to fall asleep, but as he'd admitted to Lauren, he was a man, not a robot, and the miles they'd walked, coupled with the stress of the day, had produced a weariness that pulled him under. Hidden in the trees, lulled by the vast silence and drugging heat of late afternoon, he'd slept fitfully, troubled by dreams of giant rattlesnakes and an old drill sergeant, who taunted him that he didn't have what it took to survive.

He woke with a start, the sergeant's mocking words still echoing in his ears. Gray light suffused the air around them, turning the distant trees to charcoal smudges against a washed-out paper sky. He checked his watch—almost eight o'clock.

Lauren rested heavily against his shoulder, her breathing deep and even. He buried his face in her hair and inhaled deeply of her floral and spice scent. She made him feel more vulnerable than he ever had, yet at the same time stronger. A man who had spent his life avoiding complications, he welcomed the challenges she brought to his life. She made him think beyond the next day or the next week, to what the future might look like with her in it.

She stirred and he pushed away his musings. Time to focus on the plan for right now. She opened her eyes and looked up at him, then smiled. "Does this mean the wonderful dream I was having is real?" she asked.

"What was the dream?"

Her smile widened. "It involved a big feather bed and you and me—naked."

Arousal stirred at the image her words painted. He indulged himself with a kiss—a long, slow, lingering caress of mouths and tongues that left him painfully erect and fighting the urge to take her there on the hard ground. "We'll have to see about making that dream come true later," he said.

"Promise?"

He never made promises. If you avoided them, you never had to worry about disappointing others. "How are you doing?" he asked.

"Apart from being hungry, thirsty and tired, I'm okay."

He continued to study her, his gaze almost too intense. She shifted, half turning away from him. "What? Why are you looking at me that way?"

"How long before your medication wears

off?" he said. "Before you might begin having problems?"

The question disappointed her. She'd thought he wasn't like the rest, thinking she was crazy and unpredictable. "What, are you worried I'm going to flake out on you?"

"I want to know how best to take care of you."

The sincerity in his voice made her ashamed. She stared at the ground. "Don't worry. I took a pill when we stopped for water. Before we left to talk to Prentice, I put a pill case in my pocket. It's got enough medication for a few days. I remembered the last time, when Prentice kidnapped me. He didn't get my refills for me for almost five days." She shook her head. "Withdrawal was no fun."

"I should have known you were smart enough to think ahead like that."

The compliment unsettled her almost more than his concern. "What do we do now?" she asked.

"It's almost dark," he said. "Time to make our move."

She accepted this nonanswer with good grace, and stood and brushed dry grass and leaves from her clothing. "What is our move, exactly?"

"We wait for the patrols to drive by and time

them. Even if they're deliberately trying to be random, there will be a pattern of some kind. People think and act in patterns, even if the patterns are irregular."

"It would help if we had some way to write all this down," she said.

He picked up a stick and handed it to her. "Think of the ground as a big chalkboard."

"Why bother? We wouldn't be able to see it in the dark."

Two minutes later, a distant mechanical whine cut the natural silence. Lauren peered from behind the screen of trees they'd chosen as their lookout. "I don't see anything," she said.

"They're still a ways off."

"Still, the road is pretty straight here. I'd think we'd see headlights."

The droning, mechanical sound grew louder, but the highway stretched empty in either direction. Were they driving without lights? Or did sound carry farther than he'd realized in this emptiness?

Within seconds, it sounded as if the vehicle was right on them, but still the road remained empty. "This is crazy," Lauren said. "It's like they're invisible. I thought cloaking devices were the stuff of science-fiction novels."

Marco closed his eyes and focused on the

sound. It was too high-pitched and steady for an automobile. And it wasn't coming from the road, but from straight overhead.

He grabbed Lauren and pulled her back beneath the trees. "It's not a car," he said.

"What is it?" She looked around them.

"It's a drone." He held back the branch of a tree and pointed overhead. They could just make out the shadowy shape of the unmanned drone, hovering a hundred feet above them.

"I heard Prentice had one," she said. "But I thought the feds confiscated it."

"They had to give it back," Marco said. "It's not illegal to own one. Private businesses use them for all kinds of things, from mapping terrain to aerial photography. Prentice wanted it for security patrols."

"And we're a risk to his security, so of course he's going to use it." She squinted up into the sky. "What's it doing up there?"

"Looking for us, probably."

"You mean, like, with a camera?"

"A camera. And probably infrared technology. It can map heat on the ground. Two warm bodies would be easy to spot on the heat map."

"So it can track us in the dark." She squatted on her heels and hugged her arms around her knees. "So we're toast. All the drone has to do is pinpoint us and the goons can come right to us."

"The drone can only find us if we're in the area where it's searching." Marco studied the object, which looked like a cross between an artist's rendition of a UFO and one of those radio-controlled planes hobbyists used. It made a right turn and headed back up along the road.

"But how do we know where it's going to search?" Lauren asked. "A thing like that can cover a lot of territory."

"It uses fuel like anything else, so the operators have to limit it to a defined area," he said. "I think it's making a grid pattern, searching within a hundred feet on either side of the road for five miles or so."

She stood again, and joined him in watching the craft, which was now moving away from them. "You can tell all that after watching it for a few minutes?"

"It's the plan that makes the most sense," he said. "The one I'd use if I were the operator. Prentice and his men know we have to head to the road to find other people and help. He also probably reasoned that we'd travel at night, when it's more difficult for his patrols in the Jeeps to find us."

"But the drone can find us in the dark," Lauren said. She frowned. "Is it armed? Can it shoot us?"

"There have been rumors. At one time he had a Hellfire missile with which he could have armed it, but that supposedly belonged to his Venezuelan girlfriend. She claimed diplomatic immunity and refused to implicate him. But he could have found another missile on the black market."

"What? Anyone can buy a missile?"

"All it takes is enough money and the right connections. Prentice has those."

"What do we do now?" she asked. "Make a break for it while it's gone?"

He shook his head. "The Jeep patrols are probably still near. And the drone can scan a pretty large area, even when it's not directly overhead."

"We can't just stand here, waiting to be caught—or killed."

"No." He took her hand and led her out from under the cover of the trees. "We have to turn around and head into the park."

"What's in the park that will help us?"

Good question. Black Canyon of the Gunnison National Park contained the canyon that gave it its name—a deep, almost inaccessible gorge that, while breathtaking, didn't offer any avenues of rescue. Away from the gorge lay thousands of acres of wilderness, home to everything from mountain lions to endangered birds, but very few people. The few developments in the park crowded in one corner, bordering Richard Prentice's territory. Ranger headquarters had been there, though the buildings were slated to be decommissioned and moved.

"We have to try to reach the park ranger station," he said. "We can get help there."

"How long will it take us to reach?" she asked.

"A day. Maybe two. I'm not sure how far it is."

For a moment she looked devastated, crushed by the prospect of tramping through the wilderness for two days or more. But she quickly masked the emotion and straightened her shoulders. "Then, we'd better get started."

He squeezed her hand, and they set out. Marco faked a confidence he didn't feel. What he hadn't told Lauren was that, without water and food, they had little chance of reaching park headquarters. As the rattlesnake had proved, Prentice's thugs weren't the only dangers that could kill them in the wilderness.

Chapter Thirteen

Lauren had never been so tired in her life. She had to muster every ounce of will to take each step across the rough ground. Her legs ached, her stomach hurt and only the fear of being left behind kept her stumbling after Marco in the darkness. She was so thirsty she could have wept, but she doubted she could muster the moisture for tears. How many hours had they been walking? She probably didn't want to know. The moon had risen some time ago, bathing the prairie in a silvery light that made every tree and boulder seem larger and more forbidding. Any other time in her life, she might have lay down and demanded someone help her. But Marco wasn't complaining, and he had to be suffering at least as much as she was. If he could take this, so could she.

She stumbled, falling into Marco, who turned to catch her. "Are you okay?" he asked.

She brushed her hair out of her eyes and

let out a long sigh. "I don't know," she said. "Maybe not so good. What time is it?"

"Almost midnight. Do you want to stop and rest?"

"I'm afraid if I stop, I might never get back up."

"We could try to get a couple hours' sleep."

"It's not falling asleep I'm worried about."

When he didn't answer, she looked at him, trying to judge his mood in the dim light. "Marco, if I ask you to be honest with me, you will, won't you?"

"Yes." No hesitation. He was either a very good liar, or he meant what he said. She wanted to believe the latter.

"What are our chances out here in the middle of nowhere, with no food, no water, with Prentice's men still looking for us?"

He compressed his lips into a grim line.

"Don't tell me you haven't thought about it," she said.

"Right now, I'd say our chances are fifty-fifty. If we can find water in the next few hours, those odds go up."

"I'll admit, even mud soup is sounding good to me now."

He put his arm around her. "One thing they taught us in Special Forces is that a lot of survival is mental. People survive incredible ordeals because they believe they can. Don't give up on me."

"I'm not giving up."

"Good." He clapped her on the back. "Now, what will it be? Rest, or keep going?"

"Keep going."

They began walking again, staying close together, conserving energy by walking around obstacles instead of going over them. Time was difficult to gauge, but she thought they might have walked half an hour when Marco stopped, head up, shoulders tensed.

"What is it?" she asked.

"Look at the horizon."

She looked in the direction he indicated, at the pinkish-white light showing over the tops of the trees and rock outcroppings. "Is the sun coming up already?" she asked.

"Except the sun comes up in the east, and that's north."

She didn't ask how he knew this, with no compass or map; Marco knew things like that. "Then, what's making the light?"

"That's what we're going to find out."

They moved faster now, headed toward what seemed to be the source of the light. Even hiking at top speed, they seemed to draw no closer. Lauren began to wonder if it was all a mirage.

But after another hour or so, Marco stopped again. "Listen," he said softly.

She held her breath and tried to concentrate. Past the throb of her own pulse, past the rustle of the night wind in the stunted trees, she heard a low, mechanical hum, steady and even. "What is it?" she whispered.

"Generators," he said. "You need a power source for all that light."

"But where is it?" she asked. "We've been walking for hours and we aren't getting any closer."

"Distances are tricky out here, but we're getting closer, I'm sure."

He'd said he wouldn't lie to her, but still she doubted, until she realized after more walking that the sound of the generators was getting louder. Soon they heard not just engine noises but the clank of metal and muffled voices, like a crowd of people talking.

Still, there was no sign of anyone or anything on the flat, featureless prairie, just the soft glow of light that seemed to emanate from the ground. "Are they underground?" she asked.

"Sort of," Marco said. "I think they're in a canyon. The Black Canyon isn't the only one around here, just the largest."

"I didn't pay much attention to the map the park service gave me the first time I visited," she said. "I'm not really much of an outdoors person." And after today, she didn't care if she never saw a hiking trail or a campsite again.

"Let's keep going," he said. "Stay behind me."

They moved more cautiously as they approached the lights and noises, keeping to the deeper shadows as much as possible. Lauren tried not to think about snakes. They weren't nocturnal, were they?

Marco led the way up a small rise, then stopped. She moved in behind him and looked down on a scene out of a dream. People—dozens of them, all men, milled around a well-lit compound. One group stood in orderly rows in front of another man, who seemed to be instructing them. Another group raced through an obstacle course of stacked tires and ropes. Still others zipped around the compound on all-terrain vehicles or lounged among the rows of tan canvas tents, smoking.

Most of the men wore a kind of uniform— dull brown fatigues and heavy black boots. Many of them had rifles slung over their shoulders. She blinked, trying to make sense of the images. "Are they making a movie?" she asked. She'd seen filming in downtown Denver once, and the scene below had that same sense of busyness, everything brightly lit and everyone bustling about. The action had the same feeling of unreality to it, as if everything they looked at was staged.

Marco shook his head. "I don't think so. The Rangers would have heard about it, since we're on park land."

Her gaze came to rest on something that made her sure this was all a bizarre dream. "Is that—is that a Nazi flag?" She pointed to a flagpole near the center of the compound, from which flew the familiar swastika.

"Looks like it."

"But that's crazy!"

"Some white supremacist groups have adopted it as their symbol."

"That's horrible." She shuddered and leaned forward for a closer look. "What are they doing down there?"

"I think it's a training camp," Marco said.

"A training camp?"

"Like the ones the Taliban set up in remote mountain regions to train their followers to be terrorists. But I think this one is to train domestic terrorists."

"Who would do that? And why here—in a national park?"

"They probably enjoy the idea of thumbing their noses at the federal government— a government some of these groups refuse to even recognize. Plus, though it's only a few dozen miles from a city, the land is roadless and remote. In a year's time probably a single person doesn't come here accidentally. There have been cases of whole communities of people squatting on public land for months, even years, building cabins, growing crops—legal and illegal. Our task force was one attempt to stop some trespassing, but it's impossible with so few team members and so much land."

"But someone would have seen them coming and going."

"They probably perform most of their activities at night, and only leave the compound one or two at a time. They dress like tourists and use the ATVs, so they look like recreational riders. And they've done a good job of camouflaging the camp. Check out the netting over one end of the canyon. With that and the dun-colored canvas tents, they'd be almost invisible to anyone flying overhead."

"Do you think Richard knows about this?"

"I'd bet he's financing it." Marco turned away from the scene below to look at her. "The man has made no secret of the fact that he has nothing but disdain for the government, or that some of his most vocal supporters are white supremacists and domestic militia groups. He has the money to finance this kind of operation. It would also explain his constant supply of burly bodyguards."

"Who are always young and white and perfect physical specimens." She shuddered again, remembering the men who had watched over her while Prentice had held her captive. She glanced back into the canyon, then around them. "We have to remember where this is, so that we can report it when we get to safety."

"We're not just going to remember," Marco said. "We're going to go down there."

She stared, sure she hadn't heard him correctly. "What?"

"We have to go down there," he said. "We need food, water and a phone. They have all of that."

"But it's too dangerous."

"If we leave without at least the food and water, we'll die anyway."

"How are we going to stand up against all those men with guns?"

"We have the element of surprise on our side—they're not expecting us. They think they're safe out here in the middle of nowhere. There are plenty of places to hide down there. If we can steal a weapon, it will even the odds."

As if two people against two dozen or more was anything close to even. "You're crazy."

He didn't look crazy, though. His expression

was grim, but calm, his eyes determined. "This is the kind of thing I trained for."

"But I didn't train for this." She swallowed, trying to force down the fear that made it difficult to breathe. "I can't do this."

"Yes you can." He gripped her upper arm. "You're strong, you're smart and you're brave."

His faith in her somehow did make her feel calmer. Stronger. "And I've got you on my side," she said.

"Yeah. Remember I said I wouldn't let anything happen to you."

"Is that a promise?"

No hesitation this time, and his words were all she needed to subdue the fear. "It's a promise."

ALL OF MARCO'S training had been for moments like this. He studied the encampment, noting the position of key structures and personnel. He and Lauren had to get in, get water, food and a weapon, and gather as much information about the operation as they could, all without being caught.

He led the way down the canyon, to a spot where the walls were shallow enough for them to descend, but far enough from the encampment that he hoped they wouldn't be noticed. "I'll go first," he whispered to Lauren. "Then let me guide you down."

"You'll have to. I can't see a thing after staring at all those lights."

The sides of the canyon were littered with a loose scree of pebbles and brittle shale. He dug footholds with the heels of his boots and grabbed on to clumps of grass to slow his descent. After he'd traveled a couple of yards, he turned back toward Lauren. "Feel for the steps I made with my boots," he said softly. "Lower yourself like you're climbing down a ladder. It you start to slip, I'll catch you."

She did as he instructed, and in this way they made it almost to the bottom of the canyon. Less than ten feet from the bottom, he caught the glow of an ember out of the corner of his eye and smelled the acrid smoke of tobacco. He put out his arm to prevent Lauren from descending any farther.

"Wh—?" He silenced her by tugging on her shirt, and nodded toward the spot where the end of a cigarette glowed red, a few feet from where they would have landed on the canyon floor. As his vision grew once more accustomed to the darkness, he could make out a fatigue-clad figure, sucking hard on a cigarette.

Lauren grew very still, not even the sound of her breathing breaking the silence. Marco stared at the smoking man, willing him to finish his cigarette and return to the camp.

The man tossed the still-glowing butt to the ground and stepped on it, and then they heard the metallic hiss of a zipper being lowered.

Lauren shifted, dislodging a pebble that bounced its way down the slope, the sound of its descent echoing in the stillness. The smoker froze in the act of relieving himself and whirled around. "Who's there?" he demanded.

But even as he reached for his weapon, Marco was on him. With one move, he'd silenced him forever.

He slid the rifle from the man's hand, then dug through his pockets and found a Bowie knife, a set of brass knuckles and a cell phone. He pocketed all of these and slung the rifle over his shoulder, then began unbuttoning the man's desert camo shirt.

"What are you doing?" Lauren landed beside him with a soft thud, a little breathless.

"Help me take off his clothes. The boots, too." He finished unbuttoning the shirt and shoved it off his shoulders.

"Are you going to wear them?" Lauren squatted and began untying the laces of the dead man's boots.

"No. You are."

She recoiled. "I can't do that!" Her tone conveyed her horror at this suggestion.

"You stand out too much in those feminine

clothes, not to mention a shooter could see that blond hair a hundred yards away in the darkness." He shoved the man's cap into her hand. "Put this on. Stuff your hair underneath. Stuff cloth into the toes of the boots if you have to— they're more practical for this rough terrain than your sandals. Hurry."

He could tell she wanted to argue, but she pressed her lips together and ducked her head. Silently, she collected the clothing he handed her. "Did they teach you to kill that way in Special Forces?" she asked before he could turn away again.

"Yes. And just so you know, it's not something I enjoy doing."

"I'm glad to hear it."

She started to turn away, but he touched her arm. "I'm sorry you had to see that," he said. "I'm sorry you had to be any part of this ugliness. But sometimes, surviving means doing ugly things."

She nodded. "I know. And I don't blame you, it's just… It's hard."

"And I hope it never gets easy for you." He hoped the hardness that had been with him so long he had no hope of ever leaving it behind never touched her. He'd let himself forget, for a little while, why the two of them shouldn't be together. The events of tonight had reminded him that, no matter how much he was attracted to her and even cared for her, he couldn't bring any more pain into her life. "You're going to be okay," he said. "Remember that."

"I will."

She quickly changed into the smoker's clothing. "How do I look?" she asked.

The clothes were too big and sagged on her, but that helped hide her curves. With her hair piled onto her head and mostly hidden under the cap, she could pass for a very young recruit. "From a distance, I don't think anyone will suspect anything," he said.

"They won't suspect you, either," she said. "You look like a soldier, even without their uniform."

"That's what I'm counting on. One more thing." He handed her the knife.

She stared at the blade in her hand. Eight inches long, with a carved antler grip, it looked enormous in her delicate grasp. "What am I supposed to do with this?" she asked.

"Defend yourself, if you have to. For now, tuck it into this sheath and wear it on your belt."

She fastened the knife to her belt and they set out, keeping to the fringes of activity, avoiding any other people. "What are we looking for?" she whispered.

"The mess hall or a commissary. Someplace we can get food and water."

"There are a bunch of trash cans over there." She pointed toward a line of industrial gray garbage bins, lined up outside a building. "You need trash cans near a kitchen," she said.

"Then that's a good place to start," he said.

Keeping to the deep shadows next to the row of Quonset huts, they made their way to the open door beside the trash cans. Light streamed from the doorway, and when Marco looked inside, he saw a lone man standing at a table, peeling potatoes. "This is the place," he said. "You keep watch while I go in and get what we need. Make some kind of noise if anyone's coming."

Before she could answer, he slipped into the building, and out of sight.

Chapter Fourteen

Marco disappeared inside the kitchen before Lauren could insist that he not leave her alone there in the dark. She stared after him, trying to remember to breathe, to not panic. Everything would be okay. Marco had said so. She had to believe him, right?

"Hey, dude, you got a light?"

She plastered herself up against the building and stared at the young man who had spoken. He'd materialized out of the darkness, a cigarette in one hand, his cap shoved back on his head.

"Hey, didn't mean to startle you," he said. He moved closer and wagged the cigarette. "I lost my lighter. You got one on you?"

"Uh, no." She realized her voice was too high-pitched. She forced herself to slump her shoulders and lower her voice. "Sorry."

"Oh. Too bad. I thought maybe you were hiding out over here smoking."

"No, uh, just hanging out." Inwardly, she cringed. How lame did she sound?

"I know what you mean, dude." He settled in beside her, leaning against the wall in the darkness. "Sometimes you just have to get away from the grind. I mean, I believe in the mission and everything, but these guys never let up for a minute."

What is your mission? She wanted to ask but knew she couldn't. She should find another way to get the information out of him. "When I signed up, I didn't expect there to be so much work," she said.

"Tell me about it. I mean, I came out here expecting them to teach me about shooting and making bombs and all that. Instead, they got us spending days memorizing maps and laws and studying history. If I'd have wanted to waste my time on history classes, I'd have stayed in college."

"History is the worst," Lauren said. *History of what?* "What was the name of that guy? The one they went on and on about?"

"You mean that von Manstein guy—Hitler's military strategist? Don't these guys remember Hitler lost? I mean, he was right about a lot of things, but I don't think learning his strategy is going to help us now. We've got better weapons and intelligence and everything."

Hitler? So that swastika was for real?
"When do you think we're going to get to do
something besides drill and go to class?" she
asked.

"Nobody will tell us the exact date, but I
figure we're getting close. And it's not one
mission, right? It's a bunch. Like, one group's
going to go after transportation and somebody
else is going to take out communication. It's
going to be chaos." His voice rose, excited. "I
mean, it's going to be amazing. People won't
know what hit them."

"Yeah. Amazing." Lauren felt sick to her
stomach. Marco was right. These people were
terrorists. They wanted to destroy and kill.

She glanced toward the door to the kitchen.
What was taking Marco so long? And what
would happen if he came out and the kid was
still there?

"What's up with you?" the young man demanded. "Why are you so jumpy?"

"Oh, I…I just saw one of the officers go in
there. I didn't want him to come out and catch
me goofing off."

"One of them is in the kitchen?" Her companion laughed. "What, he wanted a midnight
snack? Of the pig swill they feed us?"

"Aren't you worried what he'll do if he
comes out and finds you?" she asked.

"These old blowhards don't scare me. They like to talk a lot, but they want us to do all the work—take all the risks while they get all the glory. This close to the mission they can't afford to cross any of us in case we go running to the authorities and screw up all their plans."

"You wouldn't do that, would you?" she asked. "Run to the authorities?"

"No way! The authorities are the ones I want to stick it to. But the officers are authorities, too, right? And they don't know what's going on in my head. So I can use that to my advantage." He tapped the side of his head with his forefinger. "I may not look it, but I'm smart. I've got an IQ of one-sixty."

"You don't seem that smart to me, soldier," Marco said from behind them. Before the young man had time to react, Marco put the blade of a large butcher knife to his throat.

Eyes wide, the young man made incoherent choking noises. Lauren was almost as terrified. How had Marco slipped up that way without her seeing him? And what was he going to do with that knife?

What he did was remove the blade from the young man's throat and step back. "What's your name?" he demanded.

"Robinson, sir." Robinson brought his hand

up in a sharp salute. "Bradley Robinson, Company Two, sir."

"If I had been an enemy, you would be dead right now, Robinson." Marco didn't look at Lauren, all his attention focused on the young soldier, whose face was still blanched white. Marco's stern expression, erect posture and air of command almost had Lauren believing he was one of the camp officers.

"Yes, sir. Dead, sir," Robinson repeated.

"Instead, tomorrow at eighteen hundred hours you will report to headquarters, where you will have a chance to redeem yourself by volunteering for a special assignment," Marco said. "You are to tell no one about this."

"Yes, sir. What is the assignment, sir?"

"You will find out tomorrow. Now go, before I decide to punish you further."

"Yes, sir." Robinson turned and ran.

When she was sure the young man had left them, Lauren moved closer to Marco. "You even frightened me," she said. "When you stepped out of the shadows with that knife."

He tucked the knife into the plastic bag she now noticed he carried. "I wouldn't have killed him unless I had to," he said. "It was better to frighten him into silence."

She glanced in the direction Robinson had run. "Do you think he will keep quiet?"

"He doesn't know my name. He was so terrified he probably can't even remember what I look like. He won't say anything."

She could believe that. Marco had been terrifying. She'd known he was a strong man, not given to showing emotion, but seeing him as he'd been tonight, so cold, ruthless even, reminded her there was so much about him she didn't know or understand. "What happens tomorrow evening when he reports to headquarters?" she asked.

"If things go our way, by tomorrow evening this camp will be gone, and everyone in it arrested."

"I found out some of what they're doing here," she said. "You were right—this is a terrorist camp. Robertson told me they've been studying Nazi military history and that they've targeted transportation and communication."

"Food isn't the only thing they're cooking in that kitchen," Marco said. "They've got ingredients for significant explosives."

She wanted to ask what he'd done with the man they'd seen peeling potatoes, but maybe it was better if she didn't know. "Did you get any food?" Her stomach growled and suddenly she felt weak and shaky.

"Drink this first." He handed her a water bottle. "Then eat this." She drained half the bottle in a few gulps, only strong willpower keeping her from moaning at the sheer joy of quenching her thirst. The protein bar he'd handed her was small and dry, but it was as welcome as any meal she'd ever eaten.

"Oh, my gosh, I feel so much better," she said. Maybe part of the shakiness and terror she'd felt had merely been a lack of food and water. She was doubly grateful for the clean water to help wash down her medication. All these necessities taken care of, she looked around. The camp was much quieter now, as if everyone but a few guards had gone to bed. "Can we leave now?"

"There's one more place we need to visit," he said.

"Where's that?" Didn't they have everything they'd come here to get—food, water and information?

"Headquarters. I want to get a look at any plans they have, and see if they have a sat phone."

"Didn't you get a phone off that first soldier?" The one he'd killed.

"It's a regular cell phone. It doesn't work out here where there are no towers. If I can get hold of a satellite phone, I can call Graham and get him to work on sending a force out here to bust this place open. They're probably already looking for us, but this place is so well hidden, they might need some help finding it."

"Won't there be guards at headquarters? And more people—maybe even people working?"

"Yes, but my guess is they've been here long enough to be growing complacent. From the looks of things—the permanent structures and worn paths—it appears they've been here several months at least. No one's bothered them in that time, so they're feeling a little invincible."

But we're *not invincible*, she thought, but didn't give voice to the words. She wouldn't succeed in dissuading Marco anyway. Besides, she knew he was right. They had to get word to someone as quickly as possible. For all they knew, the mission—whatever it entailed— would take place within a few days, or even a few hours. They had to find a way to stop that from happening.

She drained the rest of the water. "What do you want me to do?" she asked.

"Let's find the headquarters building first."

The command center was easy enough to locate, since it was the area with the most activity and people, even at this late hour. People were bustling about as if it was the middle of the day, instead of well after midnight. Marco and Lauren stopped in the shadows a short distance away and studied the large Quonset hut with a row of lighted windows along one side and an armed sentry stationed at the entrance.

"Even if we managed to get past that guard, there are too many people around for us to sneak in and steal a phone," she said. "Someone would shoot us before we'd gone five yards."

"We could create a distraction," he said. "Something that would draw away most of the personnel. We could overpower the remaining guards, grab the phone and get out."

"As soon as they realize there's no emergency, the whole camp will be on us like a swarm of ants," she said. "It's not as if we can have a getaway car waiting for us."

"What about a getaway ATV?" He indicated the side-by-side all-terrain vehicle parked beside the headquarters building, the keys conveniently still in the ignition.

"That won't get us away from here fast enough," she said. "Especially if they have Jeeps or another four-wheel drive automobile."

"Still, if we get separated, head for that and take off as fast as you can," he said.

She shook her head. "I couldn't leave you behind."

He grabbed her shoulders and turned her to face him. "I can look after myself," he said, his expression just as stern as when he'd spoken to the soldier. "Promise me you'll do it."

She shook out of his grasp. "No. I won't promise that. And I'm not some scared recruit, so don't think you can order me around."

The sternness left his face, revealing a sadness that weakened her resolve in a way that bravado never could. "I'm not worth it, you know," he said.

"What do you mean?"

"You saw me back there. I didn't hesitate to kill a man. It's how I'm wired."

She would never forget how quickly he'd silenced that lone man. "You didn't murder him for fun," she said. "There's a difference. I know that."

"You're a good person," he said. "You have enough to deal with in your life without adding someone like me."

Now she was the one who needed to be stern. "I get to decide that. Not you."

He frowned. "Then, you'd better decide to look after yourself first. If things get hairy in there, I want you to run and not look back."

Maybe she would do exactly that, if it came down to it, but she wanted to believe she was better than that, that she would never abandon him. She hoped she wouldn't have to find out. "So we're really going in?" she asked.

"We have to."

"We could leave now and walk to where you could get a signal for that cell phone."

"That could take a day or more. By then it could be too late."

She bit her lower lip. He was right, of course. "I guess if we're talking about saving the country, I shouldn't worry so much about myself," she said.

"I'll do everything I can to keep you safe, but this is bigger than both of us."

She nodded. "All right. But I think the distraction idea is too risky."

He looked at the headquarters building again. The door was closed now, but the guard still stood in front of it, rifle at the ready. Through the row of windows, they could see people working at desks or milling around conference tables. "I don't have a better plan."

"What if, instead of trying to sneak in, you walked in boldly?" she said. "Act like an officer and demand to use the phone."

"The camp isn't that large. They'd know I wasn't an officer. And what are you going to do while I'm in there?"

"Tell them you're a special envoy, and I'm you're aide."

"An envoy?"

She took a deep breath. This was either the best idea she'd ever had, or the craziest. "Tell them Richard Prentice sent you."

Chapter Fifteen

Marco stared, unsure he'd heard Lauren correctly. "Do you know for sure Richard Prentice is involved with this?" he asked.

"No. But like you said before, it's a good possibility," she said. "If he is, the mention of his name is going to carry some weight. If he isn't, you'll still throw them off guard. They'll be trying to figure out who Prentice is and why you're there. If nothing else, they'll believe you're crazy and unstable, and we could use that to our advantage."

He'd learned a lot about risk assessment in various training classes—how to determine the likelihood of success in an operation, and when the desired outcome was worth the degree of risk involved. By any measure, Lauren's plan was a bad idea. There were too many unknowns—Prentice might have nothing to do with this operation, or if he did, they might not know him by that name. Worse still, the man himself might be inside that headquarters building. He'd made a habit of distancing himself from any direct involvement in his operations, but anything was possible.

"I'm sorry. I never should have suggested it. It's too risky," Lauren said. "I can't ask you to do that. Forget I mentioned it."

"We'll do it," he said.

"What? No, it's too risky. It was a crazy idea." She put a hand to her temple. "I'm tired, and not eating has my medication all off. Don't listen to me."

"No, it was a brilliant idea."

"No, it's too dangerous."

"It is dangerous. But at this point, I don't think we have a choice." He nodded toward the building. "All the activity in there tells me something big is going down, and soon. We have to stop it before a lot of lives are lost."

Two of those lives might be their own, but he didn't have to say the words out loud. He saw the acceptance of that reality in her eyes. But she pushed the fear away and nodded. "All right. Tell me what to do."

He hefted the plastic bag with the food, water and knife. "We need to hide this."

"We can stash it in those bushes." She indicated a clump of scrub oak near where they were standing.

He brushed off his shirt and straightened the crease in his trousers, then eyed her critically. "You need a little more spit and polish if you're going to pass for an aide," he said. "Tuck in your shirt and cuff the trousers."

She did as he asked; unfortunately, tucking the shirt only emphasized her curves. He frowned. "That's not going to work." He tugged at the fabric. "Maybe you can blouse it out a little."

She grabbed his arms and stood on tiptoe to kiss him fiercely. He returned the kiss, pulling her tightly into his arms and crushing her to him. Despite all his vows to distance himself from her, he needed her now more than ever—he needed her courage and her faith in him. He needed her belief, however misguided, that he was this honorable and worthy man, one who deserved the love she so freely gave.

After a long moment, they pulled apart. He continued tugging at her shirt, avoiding looking into her eyes. When he felt more in control of his emotions, he stood back and eyed her critically. "Stick to the shadows as much as you can," he said. "I'll do my best to keep all eyes on me."

"They'll be shaking in their shoes." She smoothed her hands down his arms, then stepped back. "Are we ready to do this?"

"Let's do it."

LAUREN COULD FEEL the stares of the men around them as she followed Marco up the walkway to the headquarters building. They were ten feet from the door when the guard stepped out. "Halt!" he commanded.

"At ease, soldier." Once again, Marco had transformed himself into the arrogant, authoritative commander, prepared to mete out punishment to any who crossed him. "Special envoy Henry Hoffman here to see your commander."

The guard hesitated. Up close, he proved to be cut from the same mold as the men who'd watched over her at Prentice's mansion— young, muscular and not necessarily bright. Men programmed to follow orders. "What's the password, sir?" he asked.

"The password is your head on a plate if you don't take me to your commander, immediately."

The sharpness of the words made Lauren flinch, and the soldier paled. "Commander Carroll isn't to be disturbed," he said.

"You'd better disturb him for me," Marco said. "The success or failure of our entire mission rests on the intelligence I've been charged with conveying to him."

"Y-yes, sir." The soldier backed toward the door and opened it two inches. "Captain

Peterson," he called. "Someone here to see the commander."

A second soldier stepped out to meet them. A little older than the first, and not as beefy, he nevertheless had a shrewd look of intelligence. "The commander has given orders he's not to be disturbed," he said, eyeing Marco suspiciously.

"He's a special envoy," the guard said.

"Envoy from whom?" the second man asked.

"I have vital intelligence to share with Commander Carroll," Marco said.

"Envoy from whom?" the second man asked again, his voice more strident.

Marco fixed him with a look Lauren was sure could have frozen water. Here was the moment of no return, when their ruse either worked or fell apart. "From Mr. Prentice," he said.

Freckles stood out in relief against the second man's suddenly paper-white skin. He opened his mouth to say something, then closed it. "Come with me," he said after he'd regained his composure. Not waiting for an answer, he turned and led the way through the door.

Marco followed, Lauren close behind him. She kept her head ducked, trying to make herself invisible. But they hadn't gone three steps before their escort turned and fixed her with his scrutiny. "Who is this?"

"This is my aide. Hugo."

She kept her head down, staring at her shoes. *Hugo? That was the best he could come up with? Was it because he thought she had a huge bottom?* She fought back a nervous giggle. Definitely time to adjust her meds.

The officious man must have decided she was beneath his notice, because he turned once more and hurried down the hall. She ignored the curious glances from the men they passed. Most of them were older than the recruits she'd seen on the ground, like the smoker Marco had frightened away. Only about half the men in this building wore uniforms, but they all looked grim, even worried.

Their escort knocked on the door at the end of the corridor. "Who is it?" barked a man on the other side.

"Captain Peterson, sir." He glanced at Marco. "I have a special envoy from Mr. Prentice."

The door jerked open, almost sending the freckled man stumbling into the stocky figure who now stood before him. In his fifties, with close-cropped gray hair and narrow ice-blue eyes, he stared at Marco. "I've never seen you before," he said.

"No. I'm one of Mr. Prentice's South American contacts."

Again, Lauren had to suppress a smile. What better way to explain Marco's obviously Hispanic features to this crowd of white supremacists?

"You'd better come in." The commander held the door open wider. He put out a hand to stop Lauren. "Wait in the hall, soldier."

"My aide stays with me," Marco said.

The two men faced off. Whether intimidated by Marco's superior height, his youth or the sheer force of his glare, the commander stepped back and ushered them in. Captain Peterson brought up the rear, closing the door behind him.

Carroll moved behind his desk, the top of which was almost obscured by papers, folders and a large open case, which contained what Lauren thought might be a satellite phone. "Prentice has been promising me new information for days," he said. "But I was under the impression he was going to contact me in person, not send a third party."

"He prefers to keep a certain distance from day-to-day operations," Marco said.

Carroll snorted. "Yes, and if things go south, he walks away clean. I'm not a green recruit. I know how these things operate. But I'm fighting for a cause I believe in, and that means I'm willing to take risks and get my hands dirty."

"Are you suggesting Mr. Prentice doesn't believe in the cause?" Marco asked.

"He believes. And he's done a lot to sway others to our point of view. He's shown it's possible to give the finger to the government and walk away unscathed. That's good publicity, any way you look at it. I would never question his commitment."

"Only his bravery?" Marco asked.

From his position by the door, Peterson made a choking sound. The commander's lips whitened as he pressed them together. "What message do you have for me, Hoffman?"

Lauren held her breath. They hadn't gotten this far in the plan. What message would allay the commander's suspicions, yet allow Marco to use the sat phone to call for reinforcements? How would he tell the Rangers where they were located?

Marco pulled out a chair across from the commander's desk and sat, one ankle on his knee, a relaxed, insolent posture. "First, I need coffee. It's been a long night."

The commander scowled, but he turned to Peterson. "Go get us some coffee. And have the mess send up some sandwiches, as well."

Peterson clearly wasn't pleased at being sent

on this errand, but he didn't dare argue. Shoulders stiff, he exited the room. Lauren moved farther into the corner, keeping to the shadows as Marco had instructed.

"I don't trust that one," Marco said when Peterson had left. "He's too self-important."

"Peterson is loyal, I'm sure of it," Carroll said.

"I never assume anyone's loyalty," Marco said. "Neither does Mr. Prentice."

Carroll shifted, his chair squeaking in protest. "Say what you came here to say. I don't have time for chitchat."

"Mr. Prentice wants to know what you've done to ensure the success of the mission," Marco said.

"He knows what I've done. Doesn't he read the reports I send?"

"People can say anything on paper. He sent me here to see for myself the preparations you've made."

"The men are trained and ready. We've got the manpower and the support in place to hit more than a dozen targets at once. The state will be practically helpless within hours and the rest of the country will take notice. Our success will persuade others of our power."

"People will think foreign terrorists are responsible," Marco said.

"At first they will, but once we begin our press campaign they'll see things differently. They'll realize this isn't the work of some foreign power, but of their fellow countrymen. True patriots who want to bring the United States back to the righteous roots from which we've strayed."

As he spoke, the commander's face flushed and his voice lowered to the sonorous tones of a Gospel preacher. Lauren wondered if the words were his own, or ones he'd heard repeated so often they had become doctrine. And she wondered what would make a person so dissatisfied and disgruntled that they'd subvert patriotism into an excuse for destruction and murder.

"Are you ready for a strike immediately?" Marco asked.

"We've been ready for more than a week," Carroll said. "All we need is the go-ahead from Mr. Prentice, and the acknowledgment that he's laid all the groundwork on his end. Give us the time and date and we'll make it happen."

"I'll call him and give him my report." Marco motioned toward the sat phone. "I'll recommend he give the go-ahead now."

Carroll shoved the sat phone toward Marco. "Make the call. I'm ready to get this over with."

Marco took the phone, then nodded toward

the door. "If you'll leave us for a moment, Commander."

Carroll stared. "You're asking me to leave my office?"

"I could step into the corridor if you prefer."

He shook his head, but left the room. Lauren breathed a huge sigh of relief, but a warning look from Marco kept her in the corner. He nodded toward the door and she got the message. Just because the commander had stepped into the hall didn't mean he wasn't listening, or even watching through a crack in the door.

He powered up the phone and went to stand by the window, the antennae extended. After a moment, he punched in a series of numbers and waited.

"I'm here. Yes, the trip was terrible. It took five hours to get here from the ranch house. Excellent location, though. I'd estimate ten miles from the main road and another fifteen from the park. The wash makes good camouflage and Carroll and his men have done a good job of hiding the camp. No one would guess this is a training facility."

Lauren covered her mouth to choke back a cry of delight. Marco had found a way to give the Rangers all the information they needed to find them, all while sounding like the bored messenger he'd been portraying for the past half hour.

"I'm convinced Carroll's men are trained and ready," he continued. "He wants to strike as soon as possible. Yes, all the targets—transportation and communication. With the press campaign immediately after to clarify that this is not a foreign terrorist operation, but the work of patriots here in the US."

He waited, listening. Lauren strained her ears, but could hear nothing of the response. "Yes, sir. I'll remain here to assist the commander. Thank you, sir."

He hung up the phone and looked at her. "It's done," he said, his voice barely audible.

The door opened and Carroll entered, but there was a new stiffness in his posture, a new hardness in his gaze that put Lauren on edge. She stood up straighter, and put one hand on the Bowie knife at her belt.

"Very clever, Mr. Hoffman," Carroll said. "Though I suspect that isn't your real name."

Marco blinked, but kept his arrogant expression in place. "Commander Carroll—" he began.

"Corporal Cruz, we meet again."

Richard Prentice stepped into the room behind the commander. Only instead of his usual business suit, the billionaire wore a crisp khaki uniform, a field jacket belted tightly about his waist, twin pistols in holsters on his hips. He wore tall black boots polished to a mirror finish, and an officer's cap set at a jaunty angle on his silver-streaked brown hair. He swept a dismissive gaze over Marco, then shifted his attention to the corner. "Lauren, so nice to see you again," he said, with a smile that sent a chill through her. "But I must say, that outfit doesn't become you. We'll have to see if we can find you something more flattering. It would be a shame for a beauty like you to die dressed as a common private."

Chapter Sixteen

Marco carefully set the phone aside, his expression deliberately impassive. He avoided looking at Lauren, though he sensed her fear. Help was on the way, but it would be hours before Graham could marshal his resources and locate the canyon. He and Lauren might not have that much time.

"Should I kill them now?" Commander Carroll had drawn his handgun and had it trained on Marco. His mouth curved up in a maniacal leer that sent an icy chill up Marco's spine.

"Not yet." Prentice strode into the room. The uniform he wore magnified all his most prominent traits. He'd been arrogant before; now he exuded disdain for all around him. His clipped speech had grown harsher, the words barked out like orders. Even his posture was more haughty, shoulders back, chest up, head tilted to look down his nose at everyone and everything.

He stopped inches from Marco, so that the

younger man could smell onions on his breath and the musky aroma of his aftershave. "Who did you call?" he asked.

"The FBI." Marco met Prentice's gaze with a hard look of his own. "They'll be here soon to take apart this camp and arrest you and everyone connected to it."

"They'll be too late," Prentice said. "By the time the players in their giant bureaucracy have analyzed and criticized and compromised and referred the decision up the chain of command until someone finally decides to give the orders to proceed, we will be long gone. But before we go, we'll take out all our targets. Air traffic, highway traffic, telecommunications, even the public water supply will be completely disrupted."

The door opened and they all shifted their attention to Captain Peterson, who entered carrying a tray with a coffeepot and cups. His face reddened. "Sorry I took so long," he said. "The mess was empty. It looked as if the cook left in the middle of peeling potatoes. I had to make the coffee myself."

"Forget the coffee," Carroll said. "Mr. Prentice has identified these two as impostors trying to infiltrate us."

Peterson gaped and set the tray on the desk. "Destroying everything won't win you any friends," Marco said. "Or any influence. You'll have everyone in the country hunting you down, eager to kill you."

Prentice shook his head. "Maybe for a few days, but in the chaos that follows, people will learn they can't rely on their broken government system for help. Then we'll step in to save them. To show them a better way."

"Why would they trust the very people who caused the chaos in the first place?" Lauren spoke for the first time since Prentice's arrival. She looked less pale now, and her voice was strong—defiant. Marco admired her courage, but if he could he would have told her that defiance probably wasn't the way to lull Prentice into believing she wasn't a threat. Her best hope for escape was to try to remain as quiet and invisible as possible. That would allow Marco to create a distraction and her to run away.

Too late for that now, though. Prentice turned on her. "Most people are weak," he said. "They value their comfort—their electricity, their running water, their luxury cars and high-speed internet and twenty-four-hour streaming movies—much more than they value principles or ideals. If we take those things away from them, within twenty-four hours they'll be crying and begging and welcoming with open arms anyone who can give them what they want."

"You're wrong," she said. "People will hate you if you kill their loved ones and destroy their lives."

"Some of them," he conceded. "But the beauty of my plan is that none of them will associate what is going to happen with me. An organization—the True Patriots—will claim credit for the destruction, then I will step in to rescue society. With my money and power and concern for people, and my equal disdain for all political parties, I will be their savior."

He struck a statesmanlike pose, head up, one hand with the palm flat over his heart. "After I have stepped in and used my money to restore their creature comforts, most people will be happy to do anything I want. I'll continue to preach the message I've delivered all along of personal property rights, taking power out of the hands of politicians, et cetera. But this time people will listen to me. By the time the True Patriots step forward to support me in the rebuilding efforts, people will see them in a completely new light—not as terrorists, but as reformers—people doing what is needed to get this country back on the right track."

"You're crazy," Lauren said.

He arched one eyebrow. "You would know, wouldn't you?"

Her face flushed even more, but she made no reply.

"Let me kill them now," Carroll said. "They're going to get in our way."

"I have something better in mind for them," Prentice said. He turned back to Marco. "I hear you've gone rogue."

"Then, you heard wrong."

"No? My sources tell me you resigned your commission in the DEA and stayed behind to do what—become a vigilante?"

"Disbanding the Rangers didn't stop us from coming after you," Marco said.

Prentice cupped his chin in his hand and continued to study Marco. "Yes, I'd say you are a vigilante. You fell under the sway of a beautiful woman." He nodded to Lauren. "Her delusions—part of her mental illness—led her to advocate for the overthrow of the government. Disgruntled by your treatment at the hands of your own federal employers, you were happy to join her in her efforts. Together, the two of you masterminded a series of terrorist attacks."

"What are you talking about?" Lauren asked. "You're not making any sense."

"I'm making brilliant sense," Prentice said. "If there was any flaw in my plans to this point, it was that it didn't leave anyone for people to focus their anger on. They couldn't be angry at me, the benevolent billionaire who is paying to put their lives back together. Neither can they remain enraged at my allies in the True Patriots. But some people need someone to hate. With the seeds I have already planted in the media about your unstable nature and propensity for making up preposterous scenarios, they'll be happy to turn their anger on you, and on your deluded consort."

Marco and Lauren exchanged glances. Yes, Prentice was crazy; she wouldn't get anywhere arguing with him.

"You're not going to kill them?" Carroll asked, not hiding his disappointment.

"No, I'm going to leave them alive. In the aftermath of the attacks on the state's infrastructure, they'll be found wandering in the wilderness, out of their minds and protesting their innocence." He addressed Lauren again. "Part of our media campaign following the attacks will be to place the blame for the events on you. We'll be free to manufacture whatever evidence we like, and we'll give people plenty of reasons to discount everything you say. Before you know it, you two will be the most hated people in the country." He reached out and rubbed a lock of Lauren's hair between his thumb and forefinger. "Given what I know about you, that would be a fate worse than death."

"The Rangers won't believe you," Marco said.

Prentice waved his hand dismissively. "The Ranger Brigade is already a defunct task force. Their vendetta against me prevented them from effectively performing the job they were designed to do. Any continued defamation of my character will be dismissed as the whining of poor losers."

The man clearly believed everything he said, and expected everyone else to believe it, too. The depth of his delusion was astonishing—but it also made him more dangerous. If believing you would survive increased your chances of making it out of a life-threatening situation, then believing you couldn't fail also increased your chances of success. And Prentice had already proved he was a master at swaying public opinion in his favor. "You've thought of every angle, haven't you?" Marco said.

"Of course."

Let him believe that, Marco thought. *But he doesn't know me. And he doesn't know Lauren. Not really. We didn't come this far to give up.*

"If we're not going to kill them, what are we going to do with them?" Carroll asked.

"Lock them up for now," Prentice said. "We'll turn them loose right before we leave. With no transportation or way to communicate, it will be hours before anyone finds them, or they find their way to civilization—or what's left of it."

"Where should I lock them up?" Carroll asked.

Prentice turned to scowl at him. "Don't you have a brig, or whatever it's called?"

"We haven't needed one. The penalty for most infractions is death."

No wonder the soldier who'd been caught smoking outside the kitchen had looked so terrified, Marco thought.

"There must be some building with a lock on it," Prentice said.

"Some of the offices have locks on the doors and windows," Captain Peterson offered.

"Then, find one of them to put them in," Prentice said. "It will only be for a couple of hours."

Carroll hesitated.

"Do it, man!" Prentice barked. "We don't have time to waste. Start mobilizing the men. Our mission starts now!"

Carroll shoved the pistol into its holster, then turned to Peterson. "Take them to that empty office down at the end of the hall. Find somebody to guard them. Then report back here immediately."

"Yes, sir." Peterson saluted, then grabbed hold of Lauren's arm and tugged her toward the door.

"Oww! You're hurting me," she protested.

Marco lashed out, striking the captain square on the jaw. Peterson reeled, then reached for his pistol. But Carroll was quicker. He struck Marco on the back of the head with something heavy. The last thing Marco saw before he slid into blackness was Lauren's horrified expression as she stared at him, her mouth open in a scream he couldn't hear.

LAUREN HUGGED HER arms across her chest and paced the length of the small office—five steps across, five steps back. The too-big boots Marco had taken from the dead soldier slapped against the tile floor with a muffled thud, like a rubber mallet hitting a spike.

She clenched her teeth together to keep from chattering and blinked rapidly to clear her eyes of tears she willed not to fall. She'd been alone in this room for fifteen minutes, according to the clock on the otherwise empty metal desk. Where was Marco? Had they decided to shoot him after all? She'd listened, but had heard no gunfire. She told herself this was a good thing, though she knew they might have dragged him far away, out of hearing range.

Though she heard no gunfire, sounds of activity were everywhere—marching feet, shouting voices, the roar of engines. This interior room had no windows, so she couldn't see what was going on, but she imagined men taking down tents, gathering weapons and supplies and mobilizing to spread out across the state to wreak destruction. In the past, terrorists had blown up bridges and power plants and threatened water supplies and communication centers. From what Prentice had said, his organization, the True Patriots—the name made her gag—planned to do all of this and more.

Scuffling in the hallway outside made her jump. She ran toward the door, and narrowly avoided being struck when it burst open and Marco stumbled into the room. He landed on his hands and knees in the middle of the floor, his shirt torn, one eye black, blood dripping from a busted lip. "Stay quiet in here," Peterson ordered. "I'll deal with you later." Then he slammed the door shut, his boot heels making sharp, staccato beats on the tile as he marched away.

Lauren knelt beside Marco and gingerly touched his shoulder. "What happened?" she asked.

"Peterson thought it would be fun to get

a little rough," he said. "I'll be fine." But he winced as he stood, and his breath caught as he straightened. He looked at her. "What about you?" he asked. "Are you all right?"

"I'm fine." Sick with worry and fear, but physically, she was untouched. "What are we going to do?" she asked. "How are we going to stop them?"

"The Rangers know we're here now. They'll do what they can to rescue us."

"But they'll never get here in time," she said. "Prentice was right about that. It will take hours to mobilize the officers and the equipment they'll need. From the sounds of all the activity out there, by then everyone will be gone."

Marco leaned against the desk. "We'll have to find a way to get out," he said. "We can't do much locked in this room."

"There's a guard outside the door," she said.

Marco nodded. "I saw him. A big, beefy guy with an AK-47."

"I could try to distract him with my feminine wiles," she said. "Though frankly, after two days in the wilderness, I don't look or smell very sexy." As soon as she was back in the land of indoor plumbing, she wanted a long, hot shower and a shampoo.

"You still look gorgeous," Marco said. "But

I don't want you getting near any of these punks." He straightened and began to prowl the room. "There's no window, and no way to cut through the walls."

"Is there just the one guard?" she asked.

He nodded. "They need everyone else to help dismantle the camp and distribute the weapons and explosives necessary for their 'mission.'"

"Then, if you could get him in here, maybe the two of us could overpower him."

He stopped. "That's not a bad idea." He looked around him, then picked up the desk chair, turned it over and pulled off the bottom half, with its five rollers. "I can knock him out with this. But how do we get him in here?"

"I've got an idea I think will work," she said. "Are you ready?"

"What's the idea?" he asked.

"Trust me, this will work better if you're surprised, too. Just stand over there behind the door and when he comes in, hit him hard."

He moved into position then nodded. Lauren stood up straight, took a deep breath, then let out a loud, blood-chilling scream.

Chapter Seventeen

Lauren's throat was raw and her voice was fading by the time the door opened and the guard looked in. "What's wrong?" he demanded.

"He's bleeding to death!" She channeled all the fear and panic of the past twenty-four hours into her voice, and pointed a shaking finger across the room to a spot out of the guard's line of sight. "Help!" Then she began to scream again, loud and incessant and, she hoped, annoying enough to make the guard want to do anything to stop it.

He stepped farther into the room, the rifle cradled across his chest. As soon as he fully cleared the door, Marco stepped out and brought the heavy wheels of the office chair down on his skull. With a single low groan, the guard sank to his knees and toppled over, shaking the floor with the impact of his landing.

Marco grabbed the rifle, then ripped the sleeve from his torn shirt and handed it to

Lauren. "Gag him with this," he said. He began tearing the other sleeve to use to tie the man's hands.

By the time he'd trussed the guard's hands and feet and Lauren had tied on the gag, the man was awake. He glared at them, unmoving. "Just lie still," Marco said. "Probably the best thing for you is to pretend you were out the whole time." He patted the man's shoulder, then nodded to Lauren. "Let's go."

"Where to?" she asked, falling into step behind him.

"Thanks to the guys who beat me up, I know where the back door is," Marco said, even as they reached the closed portal. He pulled it open and she found herself standing in a small, quiet courtyard containing a picnic table, a few chairs and a can of sand studded with cigarette butts. But the·space was deserted.

"Now we need to get to the mess," he said.

She stopped and stared at him, hands on her hips. "Marco, I know we haven't had much to eat, but now isn't the time," she protested.

"Not for food," he said. "For explosives."

She blinked. "What are you going to do with explosives?"

"We've got to find a way to keep these guys from leaving this canyon." He took her hand and pulled her across the compound. Half a dozen men raced past, carrying packs and weapons. None glanced their way. In other parts of the compound, soldiers loaded trucks or dismantled tents and Quonset huts. "We need to hurry," Marco said. "If we block their exit with an explosion, they'll be trapped and waiting when the Rangers show up."

THEY RACED TOWARD the mess hall, weaving through marching lines of men headed away from the camp. The Quonset hut that had served as kitchen, mess hall and commissary was deserted, the door standing open. Inside, the pile of half-peeled potatoes and the paring knife still waited on the counter, but the shelves had been ransacked, a trash can overturned, a refrigerator left half-open in the haste to depart.

A door at the back of the building opened onto a large pantry and he led the way there. When Marco had been here earlier, the shelves had been lined with canned goods and cases of MREs, the "meals ready to eat" rations the modern military relied on in the field. But in addition to food, the shelves had also held boxes of blasting caps and bins full of plastic explosives.

Those boxes and bins were gone now, as were most of the canned goods. He felt along the shelves until he came to one that was fitted behind the water heater that supplied the kitchen. Something hard met his fingertips. He pulled out a single box of explosives.

He ripped open the top of the box and they stared at a row of off-white bricks of puttylike material. Lauren took a step back. "Is that safe to handle?" she asked.

"It's harmless until you insert the detonator." He closed the box and searched the shelves for the detonator he'd need. Not finding it, he shoved the box into Lauren's arms and dropped to the floor, feeling under the shelves. As he'd hoped, a single detonator had fallen behind there when they'd swept the shelves clean. He examined the four-inch plastic tube attached to a coil of wire, then tucked it into his pocket.

"Do you really know how to build a bomb?" she asked.

"In theory, yes." He took the box of C-4 from her.

"But in reality?"

"I've never actually done it, no. Maybe you could help."

She clearly didn't appreciate his joke. She crossed her arms over her chest and took a step back. "I can't even make cake from a boxed mix," she said. "If you don't know the recipe for this particular main dish, then I can't help you."

He found an empty backpack in the debris scattered around the room and stuffed the explosives inside.

"It makes me nervous, thinking of you carrying that stuff around," Lauren said.

"We don't have time to be nervous." He added a couple of bottles of water to the pack. "We can't afford to waste a second." Some vehicles had probably already left the canyon, though these would have most likely contained scouts and other people whose job it was to do the advance work and get everything ready for the men who would set the bombs or booby traps or whatever destructive plans the terrorist operatives had made. But the foot soldiers—the demolitions experts and shooters and lookouts—would soon follow, spreading out to their targets, which, from what Prentice and others had indicated, included multiple sites throughout the state.

"Come on," he said. "We're going to have to run." He slung the pack onto his back and they hurried from the kitchen. Outside, the chaos had died down. Whole rows of tents had vanished and two of the Quonset huts had already been dismantled, the pieces loaded into waiting trucks. Only a few people worked dismantling a third hut.

"Where is everybody?" Lauren asked.

"Let's hope they haven't already been deployed on their mission," he said. He broke into a trot, moving quickly across the camp. Again, no one paid them any particular attention; they were just two more soldiers hurrying to put their training into action.

"Where…where are we going?" Lauren asked, a little breathless as she ran after him.

"They must have a way of getting all these vehicles in here." He pointed to three rows of Jeeps and ATVs parked near the command center. "They must have built some kind of ramp into the canyon. If we can find it and destroy it, they won't be able to drive out. That should slow them down enough to allow the Rangers time to get here."

"How are we going to find it?" she asked.

"We follow the vehicles." He pointed to a line of loaded trucks making their way out of camp. Most of them were smaller trucks, high-clearance and four-wheel drive to handle the rough terrain, but incapable of carrying more than a half dozen men or a few thousand pounds of cargo at a time. They rumbled along in a slow-moving line, men sitting on the sides of the beds or hanging out of the cabs, staring ahead impatiently, anxious to be on their way.

At first, Marco and Lauren raced alongside the trucks, quickly outpacing the lumbering vehicles. But as the canyon narrowed, they were forced to move to the sides, moving up the incline, weaving their way among cactus and knots of brush that slowed their progress. He kept an eye on the line of slowly moving trucks, both to gauge their progress, and in case anyone noticed them and tried to take them out.

But everyone was focused on clearing the area as quickly as possible. Most of the men would have no idea command had captured two prisoners or that those prisoners had escaped. Lauren and Marco were merely two more soldiers, hurrying to accomplish a mission they had all somehow been brainwashed into believing was the good and right thing to do.

"There are so many trucks ahead of us," Lauren said. She'd moved up beside him, doing a good job of keeping up. "We'll never be able to stop them all."

"We can stop most of them." He hefted the backpack higher on his shoulders. "The ones we can't stop, the Rangers can." One of the first things Graham would have done would have been to set up roadblocks throughout the area to stop anyone who looked suspicious. Even if Marco and Lauren didn't stop every vehicle, they could prevent most of the destruction Prentice had planned.

The trucks in line beside them had stopped

altogether now. Lauren touched his shoulder and pointed up ahead. "Look!"

A single vehicle was making its way up a narrow earthen ramp, big, knobby tires biting into the loose soil and rock. Ten feet wide, with at least a seven percent grade, the exit route was treacherous enough that the trucks could only navigate it one at a time, and slowly. One carefully placed charge would be enough to block the exit completely.

He removed the backpack and opened it, and took out a single brick of C-4. After a moment's thought, he added a second brick. He would only have one chance, so he had to get it right the first time.

"How are you going to get down there to plant the bomb?" Lauren asked. "Someone will see you right away and kill you."

She was right. Even if he had someone—and Lauren was the only other person on his side at the moment—lay down covering fire, he'd never have time to move into position and set the explosives up properly, especially given his unfamiliarity with their operation. He frowned at the ascending truck, trying to think of a way—any way—to get to the ramp unseen. The sun was up now, and though shadows still engulfed much of the canyon, sun poured into this eastern end, lighting the ramp like a spotlight.

He slipped the C-4 into the pack and carefully slid it beneath a clump of scrub oak. "You're right," he said. "Time for plan B."

She crossed her arms over her chest. "And what's plan B?"

He slipped the rifle off his shoulder and checked to see that it was loaded. "If I can disable one of the trucks while it's on the ramp, it will block the exit. It will take some time for them to move it out of the way. If I can, I'll disable several vehicles."

"And the minute you start firing, you'll have two dozen guns just like that one shooting this way," she said. "Fired by men who have had nothing better to do with their time for weeks than practice shooting."

"You're right," he said. "But I wasn't planning to shoot from here." He looked up the slope ahead of them. "We need to take a sniper's position, concealed in good cover, probably up on the rim and a little ahead of most of the men, shooting down. And we move before anyone can reach us."

"So we've got to climb," she said.

"Yes, and we need to hurry."

He put her ahead of him and took up a position behind her, his weapon at the ready, aware that if anyone in the line of waiting trucks noticed them, they might think it suspicious that they were taking this difficult route out. At the top, she stopped, bent over at the waist, hands on her knees, breathing hard, her face flushed. He handed her a bottle of water and after a moment she straightened and drank deeply.

From this angle, they could no longer see the trucks and troops below, though he could hear the idling engines and muffled voices. Lauren looked out across the prairie as she drank, squinting into the sun. "It's so tempting to just walk away," she said. "To leave the danger and go back to trying to find help."

"Doing that might mean a lot of innocent people die," he said.

"I said it was tempting, not that I'd do it." She handed him the water bottle. "Come on. Let's find a good place to hide and do this."

He led the way along the rim, keeping low as they approached the ramp. They had to descend a couple of feet to have a good view of the vehicles crawling up the slope. The first truck had almost made it to the top, in perfect position to block all of those waiting to exit behind it. Silently, Marco indicated a boulder amid a clump of scrub. Lauren nodded and moved to crouch behind it. Marco slid alongside her, stretched out with the rifle propped on the boulder. He sighted on the truck, trying to decide whether to aim for the tires or the engine block.

"It's going to be loud," he said softly. "You might want to cover your ears."

She clapped her hands over her ears, and shut her eyes as well, her lips pressed tightly together as if to bite back screams.

The first shot took out the nearside rear tire. The second round of fire peppered the front quarter-panel and hood with holes and exploded one of the front tires. Men shouted and poured out of the surrounding vehicles like ants. Several looked up the slope in their direction and pointed, and raised their rifles.

"We've got to run," Marco said. He leaped to his feet and pulled her up beside him, then retreated up and back along the rim, out of sight of the soldiers, but not out of hearing range of their shouts.

"Are they going to come after us?" Lauren asked, when they stopped in the deep shade of an overhanging rock to catch their breath.

"They'll send someone," he said. "But we'll make sure they don't find us." He slid down a couple of feet to study the activity below. Lauren moved in behind him, her hands at his waist, her chin on his shoulder. He found himself matching the rhythm of his breathing to her own, calmed by her steadfast presence.

He'd worked with many partners on various missions, men he admired and respected, some he hadn't much liked but had learned to trust with his life, a few, like Rand, for whom he felt a deep friendship, But he'd never had a partner like Lauren, someone he felt compelled to protect, yet whom he depended on to prop him up emotionally. He'd gotten through tough missions before by setting all emotion aside, becoming a robot who relied on instinct and training. Lauren made him feel everything from fear to triumph more intently; he wouldn't give up the pleasure she brought him in order to avoid the pain.

"No!" Lauren's cry, the single word half-smothered in his back, startled him.

He whirled around, heart pounding. "What's wrong? Are you hurt?"

"No, but Prentice is getting away." She pointed toward the crowd of men around the disabled truck. A single black ATV negotiated the edge of the ramp, lurching toward the canyon rim. Richard Prentice, bareheaded, with a rifle slung across his back, stood in his seat as he powered the vehicle up the slope. "We've got to stop him," Lauren said.

He was too far away to shoot at the vehicle or the man. He and Lauren would never outrun the ATV. He searched the line of vehicles waiting behind the truck and spotted a side-by-side ATV. He straightened and brushed debris from his clothes, then cradled the rifle and started walking down the slope.

"What are you doing?" Lauren asked, racing after him.

He assumed his commanding officer demeanor and marched straight toward the soldiers, who were so intent on the action ahead that they didn't notice him until he stood beside the driver. "Soldier, I need this vehicle," he said. "I'm ordering you to turn it over to me at once."

The soldier, who couldn't have been more than twenty-two or twenty-three, blond hairs sprouting from his chin and acne scars on his cheeks, gaped at him. "That's an order, soldier!" Marco barked, and hefted the rifle.

"Y-yes sir," the man stammered, and slid out from behind the wheel. His companion fell from the passenger side and scrambled to his feet, trying to regain his balance and salute at the same time. Marco slid into the driver's seat and Lauren raced around to climb in beside him.

"Hang on!" Marco shouted, and gunned the ATV forward, past the stranded truck, on the same course set by Prentice. The vehicle bucked and dipped, but made steady progress up the slope, gaining speed as they neared the rim.

"He's too far ahead!" Lauren shouted over the roar of the engine as they crested the canyon and spotted the dust trail far ahead that marked Prentice's passage.

"We'll catch up to him," Marco said, and floored the gas pedal. With two people, he had a heavier load than Prentice's machine, but the side-by-side ATV also had a more powerful engine and was more stable than the four-wheeler Prentice drove. They raced in a straight line, bouncing over rocks and cactus, swerving only to avoid larger trees and boulders. Lauren clung to the handhold, her hat long gone, long hair flying out behind her.

"We're gaining on him!" she shouted.

Prentice looked over his shoulder and saw them drawing closer. He drew a pistol and fired it in their direction, the shots wide of their mark, sailing into the scrub around them. He fired until he was out of ammunition, and then he tossed the gun aside, hunched low over the steering wheel and sped on.

"What's that up ahead?" Lauren shouted. "Where is he headed?"

She pointed to a low line of trees in the distance, taller than the surrounding growth, and interspersed with jagged piles of rock. Marco glanced at the sun. They were heading due south now. "I think it's the Black Canyon," he said. "The end that isn't along the park road."

Compared to the Black Canyon, the depression the terrorists had chosen for their camp was little more than a ditch. The steep, jagged sides of the Black Canyon plunged up to twenty-seven hundred feet to the roaring Colorado River below. The national park contained only fourteen miles of the forty-eight-mile-long canyon, though a large chunk of the rest of it was preserved in the Gunnison Gorge National Conservation Area, also part of the Rangers' turf.

But Marco hadn't spent much time exploring the canyon itself. He'd been too preoccupied with crimes in other areas of the park to pay much attention to the gorge that cut a deep slash across a large swath of southwestern Colorado. Now the remoteness and wildness of the area struck him. They'd long ago left the hubbub of the camp behind, and entered this landscape of deep silence and endless vistas, places no man had set foot in years, even centuries.

"He's not stopping!" Lauren shouted as they drew closer to the line of trees that marked the canyon's rim.

If anything, Prentice had increased his speed as he neared the rim. Did he think he could jump it? Even if his ATV had been able to clear the one-thousand-foot distance from one side of the canyon to the other, the rocks and trees that crowded the rim would have prevented him from having a clear shot. If he went over the edge, he would be dashed to pieces on the rocks jutting from the walls, long before he reached the water.

"He's going to drive right over the rim." Lauren covered her eyes with her hands.

Prentice skidded toward the rim, gravel flying up from his tires. At the last possible moment, the ATV came to rest in a tangle of scrub oaks and piñon. Prentice dived from the driver's seat and began running toward the rim. "Does he think he can climb down?" Lauren asked.

"I think he's running for cover," Marco said. "He plans to pick us off from there." He sped up the machine and took it to the edge of the rim, gravel flying from under the front wheels when he braked to a stop, ricocheting off the canyon walls as it fell.

Prentice's first shots whistled in the air around them. Marco shoved Lauren out of the ATV and dived after her. They rolled and scrambled into the cover of trees, then took up a more secure position behind a pile of boulders. Prentice continued to fire from his own position a hundred yards farther west, bullets thudding into the trunks of nearby trees or cutting chips from the rocks.

Marco unslung the rifle from his shoulder and handed it to Lauren. "Can you fire at the rocks around him, just to keep him occupied, while I sneak around the other side?" he asked.

She took the weapon and stared at it. "I don't think I could hit anything. At least not on purpose."

"You don't have to hit anything, just occupy his attention while I move into position."

She gripped the gun more firmly and nodded, her face pale, her eyes determined in spite of her fear. "All right. I will."

He shifted into a better stance to make a run for it when she started firing. She put a hand on his shoulder and pulled him back. When he sent her a questioning look, she leaned forward and kissed him, directly on the mouth and hard enough to bruise his lips. "Be careful," she whispered, then turned away, steadying the gun in front of her, ready to fire.

Chapter Eighteen

He hadn't expected that kiss, Lauren thought as she pulled the rifle's trigger and sent the first of a barrage of bullets in Prentice's direction. Maybe he didn't think this was the time or the place for kissing, but she wasn't going to let him leave her without some way of letting him know how much he meant to her.

She didn't want to think it might be the last chance she'd have to kiss him. They'd survived so many last chances in the past few days. Surely they could make it through a few more.

The gun frightened her, but as she tapped the trigger over and over she began to gain confidence. She sighted down the barrel and aimed the shots to Prentice's right or left. She couldn't really see him, only the flash of his own gunfire as he answered her. He didn't seem to realize they'd changed shooters. She'd lost sight of Marco almost as soon as he'd left her; she prayed he was all right.

Suddenly, she glimpsed him on the rocks above and behind Prentice. She held her fire and stared at him. He crouched like a tiger waiting for a chance to jump. She took her finger off the trigger, waiting.

Prentice continued to fire at her, then silence. Was he out of ammunition? Or had he finally figured out something was going on? She raised the gun and pulled the trigger again, but the response was only an empty click. She was out of ammunition. Why hadn't she made Marco show her how to reload?

She turned her attention back to him in time to see him leap, a superhero without a cape. Prentice screamed and almost immediately the two rolled from behind the obscuring rock, each grappling for a hold on the other. Lauren stood to watch, the rifle dangling useless in her hand. Surely Prentice was no match for the younger, trained man. But desperation must have given him strength. He fought back hard, refusing to surrender.

The two men rolled farther away from the sheltering rock, but closer to the dropoff to the canyon. "Be careful!" Lauren screamed. She took a few steps toward the struggling men. Prentice's face was crimson, his mouth contorted in a grimace as he clawed at Marco's face with one hand and shoved at his shoulder with the other.

"Marco!" she shouted, but he gave no indication that he heard her. His face was set in a stony expression of determination as he thrust one hand under Prentice's chin and shoved, forcing it back at an unnatural angle.

They were only a foot or so from the dropoff now. Lauren screamed as they rolled again and came to rest inches from the edge, Prentice straddling the younger man, driving Marco's head over and over again into the rock.

Lauren looked at the rifle in her hand. If they had swapped places, Marco would have saved a bullet to shoot Prentice. But even if she'd had the ammunition, there was no way her aim was good enough to be certain she could hit the billionaire and not Marco. She dropped the rifle and stooped and picked up a large rock. Maybe she could get close enough to hit Prentice in the head...

With a grunt, Marco shoved upward, hurling Prentice off him, back away from the canyon rim. Both men scrambled to their feet, legs planted, arms at their sides in a wrestler's pose. "Don't come any closer," Prentice said. "I'll jump and I'll take you with me."

"You'd kill yourself just to get back at me?"

"I'd kill myself to save the mission," Prentice said.

"The mission is already lost." Marco took a step sideways, away from the rim, but Prentice didn't follow. "The Rangers are on their way. They know about your plot. You'll never succeed. Come with me. At least then you'll have another chance to talk your way out of trouble."

"You're wrong! We will succeed!" He wore the dazed, wild-eyed expression of someone who wasn't fully present.

Marco took a step forward; Prentice a step back. His back foot teetered on the edge, loose rock falling, before he regained his balance. "Don't come any closer," he warned.

"Richard, don't do this!" Lauren could keep silent no longer.

He looked at her, his expression softening, some of the wildness leaving his eyes. "We could have been so good together," he said. "I would have given you anything you wanted. No one would have dared to say a word against you if you were my wife."

"I didn't want that kind of life," she said. "I didn't need someone to protect me." She only needed someone to love her and to accept her as she was. Someone like Marco. Her gaze shifted to him. He thought he was too dangerous and dark for her, but he didn't realize how much they had in common. They both had things they regretted in their pasts, troubles that would never entirely leave them. But they also had faith in each other. Together, they were both stronger than they were apart.

Movement out of the corner of her eye distracted her, and then a strange, animal yell raised prickles of gooseflesh along her arms. She glanced over in time to see Prentice hurtling toward Marco, a long, sharp stick held in front of him like a lance. Marco doubled over to take the blow on his shoulder, then charged forward, knocking Prentice off his feet. Marco grabbed at the older man as he fell, grasping a fistful of shirt, bracing both feet to haul him back from the edge.

Lauren would never forget the sound of the fabric tearing, or Prentice's screams as he hurtled over the edge, screams that echoed over and over through the still air as he fell.

"OFFICERS ON THE scene arrested thirty-four men and confiscated more than three hundred pounds of explosives, dozens of automatic weapons and thousands of rounds of ammunition. Roadblocks around the canyon captured another dozen men and trucks and additional explosives and weapons.

"Authorities say the group, which called

itself the True Patriots, had plans to blow up five major dams, fourteen highway bridges and five major water-treatment plants, and other intelligence indicates they had also targeted airports and telecommunication towers. Captain Graham Ellison with the FBI, a key figure in the investigation, said at a press conference yesterday if these terrorists had succeeded in carrying out their plans, the destruction would have resulted in the loss of hundreds, even thousands of lives, billions of dollars of damage to major infrastructure, and disrupted life for millions of citizens for the better part of a year. The repercussions would have been felt well into the next decade.

"Investigations are ongoing into the group, though evidence points to billionaire Richard Prentice as a driving force behind the organization, and its chief financier. Prentice died in a struggle with law enforcement while attempting to escape the terrorists' training facility."

Lauren's voice broke on the last words. She took a deep breath and faced the camera with what she hoped was a calm look. "This is special reporter Lauren Starling. For more on this developing story, stay tuned for my special one-hour report tomorrow night on True Patriots, True Terrorists."

The red light on the camera went out and

she breathed a sigh of relief and sat back in her chair.

"Great job, Lauren," her producer, Mitch Frasier, said.

"You were terrific." The regular evening anchor, Bradley Eversly, patted her shoulder. "Good to see you back on air."

She accepted more congratulations from others, then retreated to her dressing room to remove her heavy on-air makeup and change into more casual clothes. Her phone rang as she was brushing out her hair. "Hey, we saw you on TV," Sophie's voice greeted her. "You looked fantastic."

"It felt good to be back," she said. "A little strange, too. Where are you? It sounds noisy."

"Oh, Rand and I are at the airport. That's the other reason I called."

"Oh?" Lauren smoothed on pale pink lip gloss and checked her look in the mirror. She'd lost a little weight after her ordeal in the park, but she looked pretty good, considering.

"We're headed to Vegas. We've decided to elope."

"Oh, Sophie!"

"Now, don't be mad. We're hoping you can fly out and stand up with us at the wedding. Rand's trying to get hold of Marco, too, but so far he's not having any luck."

"Rand doesn't know where Marco is?"

"He said he took a couple of days' leave, but wouldn't say why. He must have his phone switched off. You haven't heard from him, have you?"

"No." A cold blackness pinched at her stomach at the words. She hadn't heard or seen anything from Marco since that day at the canyon rim. Helicopters full of soldiers and law enforcement had swarmed in shortly after Prentice went over the edge. One group had led her away for questioning while Marco had disappeared in a crowd of others. In the week since, she'd often thought of calling or texting him, but wasn't sure what to say. She told herself if he'd really wanted to talk to her, he'd have made the effort.

"So will you do it? Can you get away for a few days and come to Vegas?" She realized Sophie had continued talking to her while she'd been lost in thoughts of Marco.

"Oh, sure, I can get a few days off, now that the special is wrapped up. When is the wedding?"

"Whenever you get here. I'll call you later with more details. We have to board the plane now."

Sophie hung up and Lauren ended the call, fighting the sadness that threatened to overwhelm her. She should have been thrilled for her sister, excited about the prospect of a wedding, happy at the positive turn her life had taken. She was working again, as a special correspondent for the number one station in Denver. The public was starting to see that all of Richard Prentice's accusations against her had been false, and that he was the real villain of this tale. Though they might never prove it, the Rangers suspected Prentice was behind the threatening notes, the sabotage of her car and the other attacks on Lauren after she escaped from Prentice's ranch.

She should have been happy, but she couldn't get past this emptiness she felt. Maybe being bipolar made her more susceptible to these black moods, but she had a sense that anyone in her situation would have been blue. The man she loved was avoiding her, and she didn't know what to do about it.

She left the station and drove the short distance to her new apartment in Denver's fashionable lower downtown area. She was crossing the parking lot to her front door when a tall, muscular man stepped out of the shadows. She caught her breath and almost dropped her keys, fighting the urge to run—though whether her legs would take her toward him or away, she couldn't be sure.

"Hello, Lauren," he said.

"Hello, Marco. I didn't know you were in Denver." Amazed by her own strength and composure, she moved past him and began unlocking the three locks on the door to the apartment. Her ordeal with Prentice had definitely made her more security conscious.

"I came to see you. Can I come in?"

"Of course."

He followed her into the apartment, which had seemed spacious enough before, but now seemed too small with him in it. "Can I get you some tea or coffee?" she asked. She set down her purse and rearranged a trio of candles on the table by the door, suddenly nervous, avoiding his gaze but feeling him watching her, like a caress, hot against her chilled skin. She swallowed, trying to find the words she needed to say to him. Her feelings for him were so mixed up, she didn't know how to even begin to approach the subject.

"I don't need anything." He put his hand on her arm. "Except to talk to you."

She felt weak-kneed at his touch, on the verge of tears, though whether tears of relief, sadness or joy, she couldn't tell. Or maybe the tears were just a sign of hysteria, of her frayed emotions finally giving way. Her skin burned where his fingers brushed against her, and once again she mustered all her willpower to move past him to the beige leather sofa fresh from the showroom. She sat and smiled up at him, composed and aloof. She wouldn't break down, not in front of him. Better to let him think his rejection had not affected her than show him how much she hurt. "How are you doing?" she asked.

She had thought he would take the matching leather armchair across from her, but instead, he sat beside her, scarcely six inches between them. His hair was freshly cut, the smooth skin of his cheeks smelling of some woodsy aftershave. "I've been busy. Things shifted into high gear after law enforcement started moving into the camp. A lot of long days gathering evidence, tracking down leads. You've been busy, too, I understand."

He hadn't really answered her question, had he? He'd told her what he'd been doing, but not how he felt. She could play that game, too. "The station has been very nice," she said. "They're calling me a special correspondent. I get to work part-time, choose the projects that appeal to me. I consulted my doctors and we all decided that would be the best way to get back into work—not too much stress or pressure."

"I saw one of the promos for the special you're doing on the True Patriots."

"What a nest of vipers they are. Half white supremacists, half far-right-wingers, with a sprinkling of guys who seem like World War II reenactors caught on the wrong side. All those quasi-Nazi uniforms and flags, as if Hitler was some great hero. It's so twisted."

"The Nazi thing was mostly Prentice's idea, I think."

"Why do you think that?"

"That old picture we found, of the guy in uniform? Turns out that was his grandfather, Bruno Adel. He worked for the SS under Hitler and fled to Venezuela, where he lived under the name of Ben Anderson. Prentice spent summers with him as a kid and apparently idolized him."

"That explains all the stamps from Venezuela in his passport."

"Adel died ten years ago, but Prentice kept ties with his friends and gradually built up a contingent of deluded sympathizers whose discontent with the US government grew into this plan to wreak havoc and ferment revolution."

"From which Prentice would emerge as the new leader and power." She grabbed a notebook and began writing furiously. "I knew some of this, but we'll have to find a way to work in the new information. It's fascinating, in a very sick way."

He waited until she finished and set the notebook aside before he spoke again. "You look good," he said. He moved his hand near hers, not quite touching.

She glanced up at him, at his beautiful, tense face. "So do you." She looked away again, like someone who moved too near a fire and had to back away. "I heard the Rangers were together again."

He nodded. "We're the big heroes now. Congress is happy to funnel money our way."

"You're the real hero," she said. "I hope people know that."

"You're wrong." He took her hand at last, his grip warm and firm. She drew a shaky breath, her heart beating wildly, forcing herself to go still, to listen to his words and not think about her feelings. "I was doing the job I was trained to do," he said. "You're the one who was really brave. You started the whole chain of events that led to the discovery of the terrorists by volunteering to go and talk to Prentice that afternoon."

"I never could have made it without you," she said.

He rubbed his thumb along the side of her hand, sending tremors through her. "We made a pretty good team, didn't we?"

"We did." She put her free hand on top of

his, stilling him. "I wanted to call you," she said. "But I didn't know what to say. I caused you so much trouble, almost got you killed…"

"I thought you were avoiding me because you'd had enough violence and death to last a lifetime."

"I have, but I don't blame any of that on you. And I wasn't avoiding you. I thought you were avoiding me."

"I was going to stay away, but Rand wouldn't let up on telling me what an idiot I was being."

"Good for Rand." Still holding his hand, she scooted closer, more confident with every minute she spent in his strong, calm presence. "I think the feelings we have between us are special. We shouldn't let them go."

His eyes met hers, dark and troubled. "I've never cared about a woman the way I care about you. But that doesn't mean we belong together. I—"

"Hush." She pressed her fingers to his lips. "I love you, Marco. It's a scary feeling, love, but I've had time to think about it, and I'm determined to face my fears. I know there are some dark things in your past. There's darkness in my life, too. Neither one of us knows what the future will look like, but we can be pretty sure it won't always be easy. I have an illness that isn't going to go away. Medication can control it, but things will happen to upset the balance. We'll have to learn to deal with that, and it won't always be easy. But if you can accept that—if you can accept me—then there's nothing in your life that will stop me from wanting to be with you."

He cupped the side of her face and looked into her eyes, spearing her with a gaze full of raw need and longing. "I stopped looking for perfection in my life a long time ago," he said. "But to me, you will always be perfect."

She had no need for more words after that. The love in his eyes, the gentleness of his caress, the intensity of his kiss, told her everything she needed or wanted to know. He pulled her close, fitting her to him as if trying to pull her into him. His kiss was both tender and commanding, claiming her, burning away the memory of every other kiss she'd ever known.

When they finally pulled apart, she was breathless and shaky, but immediately felt stronger when he smiled at her. He so seldom smiled, she delighted in knowing she was somehow responsible for his pleasure and happiness in the moment. She twined her fingers in his and returned the smile. "Let's go into the bedroom." No need to be coy with him; they both knew what they wanted.

She led him down the short hall to the one

room of the apartment she had bothered to fully furnish and decorate. The cream-colored satin comforter and lace-trimmed cotton sheets had made up for the deprivations she'd endured in those days and nights in the wilderness. Marco took in the king-size sleigh bed and luxurious bedding. "Better than the bare ground in the desert," he said. "Though I wanted to take you right there, almost more than I've ever wanted anything."

"I wanted you then, too," she said. "But now I'm glad we waited." She wrapped herself around him and they shared another searing kiss, then he slid his hands beneath the soft cotton sweater she wore, skimming her ribs and the sides of her breasts, coaxing her arms up so he could tug off the top. He caressed her breasts through the satin and lace of her bra, his erection hard and insistent against her stomach.

She reached back to unhook the bra, but he stopped her and released the catch himself, tossing aside the garment and bending to take one sensitive nipple into his mouth. She arched against him as he suckled, and moaned softly, her pulse pounding. Blindly, she found the zipper of his jeans and lowered it, feeling his erection jump beneath her fingers. While he transferred his attention to her other breast, she wrapped her hand around him and squeezed gently, smiling against him as he gasped.

Together, they stumbled toward the bed and fell back onto the soft satin, helping each other out of the rest of their clothes as they did so. Naked, they lay side by side, catching their breath and letting their eyes and hands explore each other's bodies. He was everything she'd fantasized about and more—lean muscle and bronzed skin, strength and beauty honed by years of discipline and training. She traced a scar along his shoulder and another by his hip. "How did you get these?" she asked.

"The one on my hip is from a gang shooting a long time ago, when I was a teenager. The shoulder is from Iraq. I don't think about them much anymore."

"The scars inside always last longer," she said, and he stilled, his hand resting on her thigh.

She could feel him pulling away from her, pulling the shutters over his emotions and vulnerabilities. She wanted to shake him, to force him back to her, but settled for placing her palm over his heart, as if she could keep that part of him open to her.

He blinked and he was back with her, looking into her eyes with the openness she treasured. "Yeah," he said, and squeezed her thigh softly. "Those scars stay with you."

"You don't have to hide them from me." She kissed the puckered line of flesh at his shoulder. "You don't have to hide anything from me."

"I'll try," he said. "This is new for me."

"For me, too."

They kissed again, more gently, then he rolled her onto her back and knelt over her. He smoothed the hair away from her face, the calluses on his fingers snagging in the silken strands. "I love you," he said. "I didn't want it to happen, but I couldn't stop it."

"Why didn't you want it to happen?" she asked.

"Because I'll only bring you trouble."

"You could say the same about me." She slid her hands up to caress the sides of his face. "So maybe we belong together after all—two people who know how to handle trouble."

His expression softened. "Maybe we do, at that."

"Now stop talking and make love to me."

"Yes, ma'am." He executed a mock salute, then slid his hand down her body to rest between her legs, over the hot, pulsing center of her need. As he slipped his finger inside her she let her head fall back, surrendering to the onslaught of sensation that battered at her. How was it he knew just how and where to touch her, as if he was reading her mind, or merely attuned to every sensation?

As he caressed and kissed and fondled, she let her hands and lips explore his body, as well. She felt safe in indulging every desire with him, not worried about how she appeared or what he might think. With Marco, she was free to be herself, flaws and all.

When at last he rolled on a condom and slid into her, she felt as if she'd been waiting her whole life for this moment of completion. There had been other men before him, but she could imagine no other man after him. He moved deftly, stroking and caressing, balanced over her until, with a cry, she wrapped her arms around him and pulled him to her, arching to meet each thrust, making love with him, not to him.

Her release shuddered through her, and he followed soon after, their cries of pleasure mingled and fading together. They lay joined for a long time after, breathing hard, letting the sweat dry and their bodies cool.

They slid apart and she slipped out of bed to go into the bathroom to clean herself. When she returned, she thought he'd fallen asleep, but as she climbed into bed beside him he opened his eyes and looked at her. "How's this going to work?" he asked.

"What do you mean?" She rolled onto her side to study him. He lay on his back with his hands behind his head.

"This relationship. How's it going to work, with you here in Denver and me in Montrose?"

"I'm keeping my place in Montrose. I plan to spend most of my time there. I'll only be in Denver when my work requires it, for a day or two at a time. And most of my work for the foreseeable future is going to be reporting on Richard Prentice and the terrorists."

"Then, I can see a lot of you." Did she imagine the relief in his voice?

"I think you should see a great deal of me." She smoothed her hand over his chest. "In fact, I think you should move in with me."

He rolled over onto one elbow to face her. "What about Sophie?"

"She and Rand are on their way to Vegas right now to get married. He's been trying to get hold of you to tell you."

"I turned off my phone. I needed time to think."

"To think about me?"

"About us."

"And what did you decide?"

"That I was all wrong for you. That you'd

end up hating the work I do and hating me. That I should turn around and go back to Montrose and never see you again."

"But you came here anyway."

He caressed her shoulder. "Like I said, I couldn't stay away. I love you."

Three simple words, but said by him they meant so much. She buried her head against his shoulder. "I love you, too. Will you come to live with me?"

"Maybe. First, tell me more about Vegas."

"Sophie called me from the airport. They're waiting to get married until I can get there. You should come with me and stand up as Rand's best man. I'm sure that's why he's been trying to reach you."

"I'll do that." His hand tightened on her shoulder. "But there's something else I want to do while we're there."

"What? Do you want to gamble? I'm sure we can do that, too, see some of the sights."

"I want to take a different kind of gamble. You ought to know now that I'm not a man who does things halfway. When I'm committed to a mission, I give it my all."

"Marco, what are you saying?"

He slid from beneath her and turned to face her, his gaze locked to hers. "Marry me,

Lauren. We'll do it in Vegas. We can even make it a double wedding if you want."

Her heart turned over. It was a crazy idea. Impulsive. Manic, even.

Marco was none of those things, however. She couldn't think of a person who was more sane and grounded. "You really want to marry me?" she asked.

"I'm in this for life. I want to make it official."

She smiled through the tears of joy that dimmed her vision. "Then, yes. Yes, let's do it. Let's start the rest of our life together now."

* * * * *

LARGER-PRINT BOOKS!

LARGER-PRINT BOOKS!
GET 2 FREE LARGER-PRINT NOVELS PLUS
2 FREE GIFTS!

HARLEQUIN

super romance

More Story...More Romance

READERSERVICE.COM

Manage your account online!

- Review your order history
- Manage your payments
- Update your address

> ### We've designed the Reader Service website just for you.

Enjoy all the features!

- Discover new series available to you, and read excerpts from any series.
- Respond to mailings and special monthly offers.
- Connect with favorite authors at the blog.
- Browse the Bonus Bucks catalog and online-only exculsives.
- Share your feedback.

Visit us at:

ReaderService.com